CHELSEA SMILE

CHELSEA SMILE

Peter Turnbull

This first world edition published in Great Britain 2007 by
SEVERN HOUSE PUBLISHERS LTD of
9–15 High Street, Sutton, Surrey SM1 1DF.
This first world edition published in the USA 2007 by
SEVERN HOUSE PUBLISHERS INC of
595 Madison Avenue, New York, N.Y. 10022.

British Library Cataloguing in Publication Data

Turnbull, Peter, 1950-
    Chelsea smile. - (A Hennessey and Yellich mystery)
    1. Hennessey, George (Fictitious character) - Fiction
    2. Yellich, Somerled (Fictitious character) - Fiction
    3. Police - England - Yorkshire - Fiction
    4. Murder - Investigation - England - Yorkshire - Fiction
    5. Detective and mystery stories
    I. Title
    823.9'14 [F]

    ISBN-13: 978-0-7278-6494-9 (cased)
    ISBN-13: 978-1-84751-003-7 (trade paperback)

All Severn House titles are printed on acid-free paper.

Typeset by Palimpsest Book Production Ltd.,
Grangemouth, Stirlingshire, Scotland.
Printed and bound in Great Britain by
MPG Books Ltd., Bodmin, Cornwall.

For A & KH

of

EH3

One

Monday, 2 June, 11.30 hours – 17.45 hours
in which one becomes three.

T he house was called Apsley – Apsley House. George
Hennessey halted his car at the gates and read the
name: 'Apsley' carved deeply into the stone of the left-
hand gatepost and 'House' carved equally deeply into the
stone of the right-hand gatepost. The name surprised him,
because the documentation had referred to the family
living at the more modest-sounding address of thirty-two
Hawkridge Road, York. The name also had a familiar ring
to it; it seemed that he had heard the name before, seen
it written before, somewhere. He said so.

'Does have a familiar ring to it, aye.' Yellich stared at
the gatepost and then at the driveway leading up to the
house, then the house itself: a neat, he thought, rather than
a rambling nineteenth-century building, with a lawn as
large as a football field in front of it, and surrounded by
an estate of the least expensive houses in the city.

Hennessey made no further comment but drove his car
up the drive and stopped in front of the main door. He
and Somerled Yellich got out and walked up the steps.
There was no brass knocker or doorbell, only an ancient
bell pull. Hennessey took hold of the metal ring and
pulled it twice, causing bells to jangle loudly in the interior. They stood in silence, Hennessey glancing at the

1

house, searching for period detail, Yellich turning round and looking back over the expanse of lawn towards Hawkridge Road.

Hennessey was about to pull the bell again when he heard within the house a soft but distinct footfall that was clearly approaching the door. Yellich similarly heard it and turned round to face the door. A heavy bolt was heard drawing across the doorframe and the door opened, smoothly and silently, despite its size and evident weight. An elderly woman in a grey tunic stood there, not speaking for a moment. Blinking her eyes against the sun she eventually said, 'Yes?'

'Chief Inspector Hennessey and Sergeant Yellich. We phoned earlier. We'd like to see Mrs Margaret Percival.'

'Ah . . . yes . . .' The woman stood aside. 'Please, come in; I'll tell Mrs Percival you are here.'

Hennessey and Yellich entered the cool of the building, Hennessey sweeping his panama from his head as he did so. There were seats in the foyer of the house, surrounding a long coffee table. The maid gestured to them as she closed the door. 'Please,' she said, 'do take a seat,' and walked away to the right down a corridor. Hennessey and Yellich sat as invited.

The maid returned and asked the two officers to follow her. She led them back down the corridor and up a small staircase to a doorway, upon which she knocked, then waited until a female voice said, 'Come.' She opened the door, said, 'The police, madam,' and stood aside as Hennessey and Yellich entered.

The small staircase belied the size of the room in which Mrs Percival sat. It was, the officers saw, a rectangular room, long and narrow with a single window pane that Hennessey thought was probably twelve feet high, at the further end; original glass too, he thought, noticing where the glass, being liquid, had begun to settle in places. The maid shut the door behind her as she left the room.

'Do take the weight off your feet, gentlemen.' Margaret Percival opened her palm and indicated the vacant chairs in the room. She was a middle-aged lady, Hennessey observed, with short-cropped hair and soberly dressed in blue – blue blouse, blue skirt, which hung below her knees, and lightweight summer shoes, also in blue. 'So, my dear husband is now deemed to have been murdered? I confess I was astounded at the verdict; it's been more than five years since he was attacked. I thought there was a year-and-a-day rule? I seem to remember that.'

'It used to be the case.' Hennessey held his panama gently by its rim and noticed Yellich take his notepad from his pocket. 'From medieval times. I believe it was the law that a victim of assault could not be deemed to have been murdered unless he died from his injuries within one year and a day of the attack.'

'Yes, that's what I understood.'

'The law changed a few years ago . . . now there is no time limit,' Hennessey explained. 'Too many people were escaping justice because advances in medical science were keeping victims of violent crime alive for years before they eventually succumbed, and if felons were convicted at all, they were convicted of assault but escaped a murder conviction. So the law was changed – a move with the times. Following the coroner's ruling of "Murder by person or persons unknown", your late husband's death has become a murder inquiry.'

'You are reopening the case?'

'It was never closed, Mrs Percival; it has always remained open – allowed to go cold, perhaps, but never closed – and now has been reclassified from one of grievous bodily harm to one of murder.'

'I see . . . It might have been murder five years ago for

all the man he was after the attack . . . "A shadow of his former self" is just not the expression. Requiring constant nursing care, no control of his bodily functions . . . not being able to communicate . . . a pleading look in his eyes, begging me to end it all for him. He had insight, you see, Mr . . . Hennessey?'

'Yes, Hennessey . . . like the brandy but with an extra "e".'

'That will make it easy to remember . . . like the brandy but with an extra "e" . . . But my husband: it would have been merciful if they had killed him. You know all the details of the attack?'

'Yes, it's all documented. The purpose of our visit is twofold: it is to notify you of our renewed involvement and also to ask if you have any thoughts, ideas – if anything has come to light over the last five years, anything that you may feel is relevant.'

'Oh . . .' Margaret Percival reclined in her chair. 'It's difficult to think what . . . I told the police everything all those years ago. He was definitely targeted, though: it was a well-planned attack. He wasn't a random victim . . . someone who was in the wrong place at the wrong time; and that's the mystery of it . . . not robbed . . . someone wanted him dead . . . but who and why? Well, they've got what they wanted. Had to wait, but they got what they wanted.'

'Where is the cottage?'

'It's in the Vale. Not far, really. As weekend cottages go, it's not far at all, but Duncan couldn't be dragged from Apsley or "number thirty-two", as we preferred to call the house, and as I shall still call it.'

'Yes . . . we commented as we arrived that the name did seem familiar.' Hennessey inclined his head.

'So it should.' Margaret Percival smiled. 'It was the name of the Duke of Wellington's house. The house – his

4

house – was also referred to as "number one, London", apparently because it was the first house one encountered on the London side of a tollgate.'

'Ah . . .' Hennessey and Yellich nodded to each other.

'We didn't like it – the name I mean – though we loved the house; but as you have seen, the name is carved an inch deep in the stone gateposts so we are stuck with it. Some sycophant's notion of hero-worship, or so we assumed. We thought of concreting the name over but decided against it; we thought it would look unsightly. After a while we didn't notice the name and always insisted on thirty-two Hawkridge Road as being our address. But houses with the names of other houses are not unknown. There is a Buckingham House in Leeds – it's a clear reference to the palace – and in Rotherham . . . Do you know Rotherham?'

'No, I'm from London originally; I only really know York.'

'Never been there,' Yellich replied in response to an enquiring look from Margaret Percival.

'Well, there used to be a large house in that town called "Thundercliffe Grange", as in *Wuthering Heights . . .* that is two others I know of. So houses which share the name of another, more famous house are, as I said, not unknown. The house used to have more extensive grounds. Previous owners sold off the greater part of the grounds to a housing developer, leaving only the large lawn at the front, and a small amount of land at either side and at the back. So it's a big, old house in a sea of small, new houses. I think it's called "backfill" or "infill" or some such, when the space between older properties is filled with suburban development.'

'I see . . . so . . .'

'Yes, we digress.' Margaret Percival smiled a warm smile.

'Mr Duncan Percival was attacked in the weekend cottage?'

'Yes.' Mrs Percival nodded, with clenched teeth. 'I found him. I had driven into the village to obtain some provisions . . . little things . . . we had run out of milk, I remember. Strange how small details remain in your mind, but I remember that day with such clarity.'

'You would – it's quite normal; traumatic events do imprint themselves in your mind and the smallest details are often remembered.'

'Well, I returned to the cottage . . . Lovely summer's afternoon, a day like today except it was later in the year . . . July, in fact . . . so five years ago next month. The door was open – that was the first unusual thing. Duncan always liked the door closed; he felt ill at ease with the cottage door open and so it really was quite odd to halt the car in front of an open door. Anyway, I went in, calling his name, and there he was, folded up in the living room, his face and head a mass of blood. His cheeks had been cut open and there was blood on the walls . . . furniture in disarray . . . There had been a real fight. He was a large man, getting on in years but still with a lot of strength. He would have gone down fighting . . . and no, I know of no one who would want to harm him. We lived quietly.'

'And you saw nothing before or after the attack that you might have thought relevant?'

'As I told the police at the time, nothing, and I was absent for less than half an hour.'

'Yet it was a sustained attack?'

'Yes, that has puzzled me. They . . . I am sure there was more than one . . . I mean, to be able to overpower him and do that to his cheeks . . .'

'He being well built and strong?'

'Yes, that's what I mean. They must have been observing

the cottage . . . waiting for the opportunity to strike; they must have been very confident of doing the deed before I returned. I mean, they must have known that I wasn't going far . . . I wasn't carrying any bags – just walked out of the cottage, got in the car and drove away towards the village. It was too late in the day to be going any further. Either that or it was just the purest of coincidences that they arrived when they did. A few minutes earlier or later and I would have been involved . . . and possibly not here now. So it's more comfortable for me to assume the former to be the case. I don't like to dwell on the latter possibility.'

'I can understand that.' Hennessey held eye contact with her.

'So I saw nothing, I couldn't provide the police with any suspects. He was a quiet-living retired businessman.'

'What business was he in?'

'Many and varied. He was Mr Fix-It . . . Mr Ten Per Cent. He would have described himself as a venture capitalist, though I never really asked and I was never a part of his work. I was a stay-at-home wife . . . not a kept woman, though – there is a lot of work involved in running a house this size. We have Tessie, the maid, whom you have met, and a cook, Mrs Lee, who comes each weekday to prepare lunch; but when Duncan was working we had two cooks, three maids, and also employed a part-time gardener – all had to be supervised: I was a busy woman in my own modest way – and then, after the assault . . . hired nursing care for my husband.'

'I see. So no enemies . . . that you know of?'

'That I know of,' Mrs Percival echoed.

'Who would benefit from his death? Anybody?'

'No one. I am the beneficiary of his will . . . but I would rather have a husband. I am getting on in years now . . .'

'I don't wish to be indelicate, but . . .'

'Forty-seven. I am forty-seven years old.'

'Your husband . . .?'

'Was older than me. Yes there was an age gap, so much so that we were often taken for father and daughter. He was nearly seventy when he died . . . sixty-five when his life ended in any and every meaningful way, and I was forty-two when my marriage also ended in every meaningful way. We had no children. We did try, of course . . .'

'Yes.'

'So now you will plunge further into my husband's background. I confess the police didn't seem to investigate far. I was visited and the officer told me that they just kept coming up against brick walls: no fingerprints at the scene; no enemies in the woodwork; no witnesses.'

'That may be the case still.' Hennessey spoke solemnly. 'We can make no promises, but a murder has been committed; we will have to investigate.'

'Thank you, Chief Inspector.' Again she smiled a very warm smile. 'I appreciate it and I know Duncan would appreciate it also. He hated loose ends and unfinished business.'

Thompson Ventnor accepted the mug of tea offered him by George Hennessey and sat back in his chair. He glanced to his right out of the small window in Hennessey's office and saw the ancient walls of York, gleaming in sunlight, thronged with tourists. Yellich sat on the other side of him, also cradling a mug of steaming tea.

'Can't seem to think without tea.' Hennessey put his mug down on his desk and sat in his chair, resting his elbows on the desk top. 'So, Thompson, Duncan Percival.'

'I remember the case well . . . not surprised to hear he

has succumbed . . . dreadful injuries; the medics didn't think he'd live for more than a few hours, but he proved to be a strong old boy with a real will to live.' Thompson Ventnor was short for a police officer, broad-chested, in a grey lightweight summer suit, with a moustache and well-groomed black hair. 'I didn't dig very far . . . no witnesses, no latents. He, or they, came, did the business and left again, all within a thirty- or forty-five-minute time window that was created by Mrs Percival driving into the nearest village to get some food – or something similar.'

'Any suspects?'

'Well, "Look at the in-laws before you look at the outlaws" being the rule, we did consider that Mrs Percival might have had a hand in it – paid some thugs to do her old man in, deliberately creating the time window to provide the opportunity.'

'But . . .?' Hennessey sipped his tea.

'But we abandoned the idea. Her grief seemed genuine, her shock – and she was soon demanding the best of care for her husband. That seems to have stood the test of time: she has been loyal to him over the last five years . . . despite him being virtually a vegetable.'

'Fair enough.'

'So, even though she would have done well for herself out of his death in terms of wealth, we decided not to leave her in the frame and to turn our attention to the outlaws. We seemed to have more luck there but didn't even get close to an arrest.'

'Luck, you say? What luck?'

'Well, luck is perhaps the wrong word, but we did find out about Percival's business dealings. Not all of them were kosher.'

'Really?'

'Really. The crims knew him well; he was believed to

have bankrolled some serious crimes, armed robberies – particularly armed robberies. He was close to an extortion racket . . . controlled substances . . . he was just an arm's length away from all that but never got his fingers dirty – hid behind his legitimate front as a venture capitalist. He also had a used-car business and a small bookmaker's.'

'Both very useful for laundering money,' Hennessey growled.

'That's what we thought. We were at the stage of questioning known criminals, looking for someone with a grudge, just getting a wall of silence – the "thieves' honour" number. We were getting nowhere: no break, no lead – nothing . . . and then the Saffer murders took place.'

'Oh, yes . . . elderly couple . . . blown apart by a shotgun. I worked that case as well . . . Julia and Julian Saffer.'

'I was on it too,' Yellich added.

'Well we all were – very high-profile case; all resources were put on that investigation, including me. Sharkey took me off the Percival assault and I joined the Saffer inquiry team. That case took a long time to wrap up, as you'll recall . . . but eventually it was wrapped up and we got a conviction.'

'Tom White – wasn't that his name?'

'Yes, sir.' Ventnor nodded. 'Tom White, farm labourer, lived quite close to the Saffers, in the frame at the beginning, then eliminated.'

'Yes . . . then the case began to cool.' Hennessey sat back. 'I remember now . . . then we got a tip-off, the good old anonymous phone call . . . led us to a lock-up, the murder weapon with White's prints on it, valuables he'd stolen from the Saffers' house – enough to convict him. He would have got a lower tariff if he had pleaded guilty, but, as my son is wont to say, he went NG, collected life times two with a twenty-year tariff. He'll be in his forties when he gets out. What a way to spend the greater part of your twenties, all your thirties and the first few years of your forties . . . just a stupid, senseless murder.'

'Indeed.' Ventnor drank his tea. 'But it did take a long time to get to little Tommy White – all five foot two of him . . . and we probably would not have got there at all had it not been for the phone call tipping us off about the lock-up. But after he was collared and remanded, the Saffer murder-inquiry team was dispersed to previous duties. I dusted off all my outstanding inquiries, one of which was the serious assault on Duncan Percival. By the time I did pick up the case again the wall of silence seemed to have got even higher, the case got colder . . . then new crimes were reported and eventually, the Percival case was confined to the cold cases, where it remained until last week. It's now a murder investigation.'

'As you say . . .' Hennessey glanced out of his office window. 'So how long did you investigate the Percival assault before you were pulled off to help with the Saffer murders?'

'A matter of days. The double murder of the Saffers followed hard on the heels of the Percival assault. The Saffer case took six months; so when I did return to the Percival case, it was well chilled.'

'Any connection between the two?' Hennessey spoke softly and a hush fell on the room as Yellich and Ventnor glanced at each other, then at Hennessey.

'Not at the time, skipper.' Yellich drained his mug.

'No connection at all was made.' Ventnor nodded in agreement.

'And with all the advantages of hindsight?' Hennessey shrugged his shoulders.

'Well . . .' – Ventnor shook his head – 'both occurred at the same time, both involved an extreme level of violence, both houses were in similar locations – a rural setting – but one involved a firearm, the other didn't. Percival wasn't robbed; the Saffers' house was ransacked . . . so I don't know, sir . . .'

'I can't see Tom White causing those injuries to Duncan Percival, boss,' Yellich offered. 'Tommy White is just over five feet tall; Duncan Percival was a bear of a man.'

'Unless Mrs Percival was right and there were more than two of them – Tommy White and two others . . . enough to overpower Duncan Percival. I want you with us on this one, Ventnor.'

'Yes, sir.'

'Are you busy at the present?'

'No more than usual, sir.'

'Well, this is a murder inquiry, so it takes priority. I'll clear it with Commander Sharkey.'

'Yes, sir.'

'Find out where White is.'

'Yes, sir.'

'Go and see him . . . both of you.'

'Yes, boss.'

'You can do that this afternoon. Listen to what he says, get a feel of him.'

'Yes, sir.'

'I am going to visit the scene of the attack on Duncan Percival. I'll get a feel of that. Rendezvous here at nine a.m. tomorrow.'

Thomas 'Tommy' White revealed himself to be a slightly built, nervous-looking young man who looked even smaller than he needed to, thought Yellich, because his blue striped shirt and his jeans were too large for him. It was perhaps the case that Full Sutton Prison just did not cater for the smaller man. He had short black hair, a pointed nose and a weak chin. His eyes were blue and as cold as steel. This man, Yellich saw, had hatred burning within him. Yellich took a packet of cigarettes from his jacket pocket and offered him one. White snatched at it greedily and leaned forward, putting the tip to the flame of Yellich's lighter. White drew the smoke into his lungs, held it for a few seconds and then exhaled slowly through his nostrils.

'You like a smoke, Tom?' Yellich put the cigarettes and the lighter back into his pocket.

White shrugged. 'Didn't smoke until I got banged up. Now it's my only source of fun . . . only source of pleasure.' He had a strong Yorkshire accent. 'So who be thee – cops? I can tell that; but I don't know thee.'

'Detective Sergeant Yellich, and this is Detective Sergeant Ventnor, from Micklegate Bar Police Station in York.'

'Aye?' White eyed the officers with his piercing and suspicious-looking eyes.

'Just for a chat.' Yellich relaxed as best he could in the hard upright chair. He glanced at the cream-painted walls and the solid block of opaque glass that allowed natural light into the room.

'It's why I like getting visits by cops and solicitors.' White seemed to follow Yellich's gaze. 'Yon glass – it's one of the few sources of natural light . . . that's sort of valuable to a country lad like me. There's a bloke in here, transferred him from Durham. When he was in Durham he was allowed to keep a couple of birds in a cage in his cell . . . They got sick and died. No natural light for them, you see. He's got natural light in his cell here, but he won't keep no birds again. His life was falling apart and his budgies dying was the last thing he needed.'

'You have a solicitor visiting?'

'Yeah, got an appeal lodged.' White allowed himself a brief smile. Neither officer thought it a particularly practised expression.

'Against conviction or sentence?'

'Conviction,' White answered with a certain finality. 'You know the game: you can only appeal one or the other. If you accept conviction, you can appeal against the length of sentence; but I don't accept conviction.'

'Not guilty?'

'Yep – but in here I'm classed as "Idom".'

'In denial of murder?'

'That's the prison line. They tell me, if I was to accept guilt, I could begin to work for myself; I could get a move from a Category A to a Category B prison – get away from all the hard men, all the psychopaths . . . all the serial killers and multiple rapists; get amongst crims who are working to get on the outside; get to be part of that team. Their acceptance of their guilt and willingness to cooperate with the prison system would rub off on me . . . so they say . . . it would change my attitude, get me an easier ride.'

'You won't do that?'

'No.' Again the steel-cold, piercing blue eyes fixed on Yellich, then moved to Ventnor and then back to Yellich. 'I'm innocent, see?' He paused. 'First I knew about it was when the police hammered on my door at seven o'clock one morning.' Again he paused, as if reliving the event. 'From that point my life changed. It's now like up to that point belongs to a different life – not just a different part of the same life, but another life entirely . . . but I am not accepting guilt so as to get out earlier. The judge set a minimum tariff of twenty years anyway . . . Category A, B or C. I'll be well finished by then; the old lags in here say you can't survive more than ten years

14

without being broken. If you want to survive once you're on the inside, you've got to get out in less than ten years.'

'The tariff was because you pleaded not guilty.' Ventnor spoke softly. 'That can be the first thing to appeal, if you accept your guilt.'

'So my brief says, but I am not going down that road. Is that why you are here – to buy off my appeal against sentence? – because if I win my appeal, I'll make you people look stupid? You don't mind unsafe convictions; you don't mind them at all so long as no one finds out about it . . . Then you get to look bad. A murder is done – what's the term? – high-profile. A high-profile murder and someone gets sent down for it – doesn't matter if the person is innocent; you don't care about that, so long as someone is seen to be convicted.'

'Sorry you feel that way, Tom.'

'So why is it you're here?' He drew angrily on the cigarette.

'To see what we see,' Yellich answered.

'To hear what we hear,' Ventnor added.

White sat back in his chair and smiled for the second time. 'You're not telling me that you might be on my side? You might actually be believing me?'

'We might . . . we might not . . . but you were convicted on strong evidence: the gun had your prints on it.'

'That's because I touched it, fool that I was. I heard about the old couple getting blown apart but never connected it to the shotgun I found in my lock-up.'

'You didn't?'

'No, I didn't. It was the country; everybody has a shotgun in the country. I had a lock-up at the edge of our village . . . Lots of lock-ups there . . . Just a wooden shed really, one padlock on the door . . . Kept tools there . . . working boots . . . It's cleaner than bringing them home

15

to my little council house. So I found my lock-up had been broken into, all my tools stolen but a shotgun had been left there . . . really nice gun. I thought some idiot had broken into my lock-up one night to steal my tools but had left his gun behind by mistake . . . burglars often do stupid things – forget themselves in their fear. I thought that by the time he'd realized he'd left his gun behind it was too late. Anyway, the gun was more valuable than the tools he'd taken so I thought, fair enough. Hid the gun, reported the theft to the police so I could claim the insurance, then repaired the lock . . . put the gun back in the lock-up intending to sell it.'

'You have a licence to own a firearm?'

'No, but . . . The countryside . . . somebody would have bought it.'

'The valuables?'

'Well small, easily hidden; they were in an old sack shoved into the corner of the lock-up. I didn't notice them. They may have been valuable but they were easily hidden. Not like they were oil paintings or anything like that. Someone put the shotgun and the jewels in my lock-up. I was fitted up.' He stubbed out the cigarette.

'Who'd do that to you? Know anyone who'd want to do that?'

'The person who killed that old couple, that's who.'

'And you have no alibi?'

'No. I lived alone in a little council house on the edge of East Rushton; it was my parents', but I took over the tenancy when they died.'

'You're a young man to have lost both parents.'

'They were both getting on a bit when I was born. I always got taken for their grandson when we were out. We would pretend to be just that after a while – granddad and grandma taking their grandson to the coast for a holiday. It was better than correcting people all the time.

Anyway, I was home alone when the elderly couple were done in . . . murdered. Didn't take long for the police to come to my door – two or three days . . . and I have a record for violence and I lived near them. They lived in a big house in West Rushton about half . . . no . . . nearer a mile . . . then they left me alone and came back six months later.'

'Two convictions for assault – we read the file.'

'Two fights in the Ram's Head in East Rushton – and I didn't pick either of them, but I got done for both.'

'It still didn't look good. The jury must have felt they returned the correct verdict when they heard about your track.'

Tommy White shrugged. 'Suppose they did, but it was a classic set-up: plant the jewels from the robbery in my lock-up, plant the murder weapon knowing I'd pick it up and leave my prints all over it – but who'd want to set me up? OK, I've got a few people don't like me, but not enough to see me put away for life and run a risk of being prosecuted themselves for doing so.'

'Did you know the Saffers, Tommy?' Yellich offered White another cigarette. It was snatched greedily. Yellich ignited his small disposable lighter and held the flame towards Tommy White.

'The Saffers?' Tommy White inhaled deeply as he lit the cigarette and then settled back in his chair, once again exhaling through his nose. 'Knew *of* them more than knew them.'

'Knew *of* them?'

'Well, big family in West Rushton – and East Rushton too. Did some work for them once . . . not directly for them, but I was a labourer working for a landscape gardener's: Springwell Landscapes. They were employed by the Saffers to reshape their garden and Springwell Landscapes employed me and a couple of others for the duration of the job, which took about four weeks. So I was just one of the crew, another guy in overalls digging their garden. We never spoke, not once . . . but the prosecution made something of that job. I knew the layout of their garden. All added up to that posh cow with pearls round her neck standing up and saying "Guilty", and saying it like she was pleased to say it.' He looked down at the table top.

'I see.' Yellich and Ventnor glanced at each other and raised their eyebrows. 'Do you know Mr and Mrs Percival?'

'Percival?'

'Percival – Mr Duncan Percival and Mrs Margaret Percival, his wife. They live in York but had a house in the Vale.'

Tommy White shook his head. 'Can't help you there. Sorry, not a name I know. Two houses.' He shook his head. 'Not the sort of folk I'd be knocking about with – me with my little council house.'

'OK, just floating a question.' Yellich took the cigarettes from his pocket and pushed the packet across the table to Tommy White.

'For me?' White's jaw dropped.

'Yes . . . why not? We might be back.' He stood. Ventnor did the same.

'You *are* believing me?'

'We don't disbelieve you.' Yellich tapped on the door of the agent's room. The door was opened instantly with a rattle of keys.

Yellich and Ventnor walked out of Full Sutton Prison towards the car park, both squinting in the glare of the sun. They reached Yellich's car and, after Yellich had unlocked it, opened the doors and wound down the windows, allowing the vehicle to 'breathe' before they sat in it.

'You know' – Ventnor rested his forearms on the roof of the car – 'you know, I half-believe him.'

'You've been a copper too long.' Yellich smiled. 'Only half-believe him? I do believe him.'

'You do?'

Yellich nodded. 'You see, the thing that swings it for me is the jewels. Robbing the Saffers only to hide what it was that was taken where they knew we'd find it – that's the action of someone or some persons wanting the Saffers dead and wanting someone else to take the consequences. Robbery was not the motivation for the Saffers' murder. And him' – Yellich pointed to the prison – 'not a man who is going to make much of a mark on life. He won't mark his passing with anything positive or remarkable, but he's got more about him, more common sense than to bring a murder weapon and the proceeds of a robbery back to his lock-up. He's right – he was right all along: he's been fitted up. Just a little nobody, good only to take the blame.'

'So we've got another murder to solve?'

'Two.' Yellich glanced upwards at a white vapour trail leading across the blue and near-cloudless sky – an airliner, making its way west from Continental Europe to North America, doubtless with the passengers occupying the window seats enjoying a panoramic view of the green-and-pleasant. He lowered his eyes and looked at Ventnor. 'Two: the Saffers were a double murder, but yes, another investigation, which was not linked at the time, but the boss will be right. I've worked with him a long time; he has a nose for such things: the attack on Duncan Percival and the murder of Mr and Mrs Saffer will be linked . . . and the laddie in there – well, he's racking up compensation, because he is as chaste as the unsunned snow.'

'Who said that?'

'Shakespeare.' Yellich smiled. 'My wife used to teach English Literature before I dragged her off to a cave

19

marked "Marriage – females for the disposal of", but she's always quoting stuff and I remember it . . . sometimes.'

Hennessey steeled himself against the ordeal of driving and travelled to what had previously been the Percivals' weekend cottage in Aldworth St Mary. It revealed itself to be a squat, whitewashed building of modest proportions, two windows either side of a central door below an upper floor with three windows. It stood side on to the road. Hennessey opened the gate, which creaked as he pushed it, and the sound caused a large-sounding dog to bark within the cottage. His feet crunched the gravel path, causing the dog to become even more agitated. The current owner was evidently well protected against intruders. No expensive burglar alarms needed here, mused Hennessey. He walked to the front door, saw that the building had been called 'Sundowner', took the metal knocker and rapped it twice, then paused; then knocked a third time. The door had been painted a pleasant shade of light blue and Hennessey thought the colour gelled well with the whitewashed building and the dark-slated roof. It was sensitive to the rural area, unlike a yellow or a red door might have been. The door was opened by a slender but muscular man who held a barking Labrador by its collar.

'Police?'

'Yes.' Hennessey showed his ID. 'Nothing to worry about – just making inquiries. DCI Hennessey, Micklegate Bar Police Station.'

'Knew it was the police – that knock: tap, tap . . . tap . . . the classic police officer's knock. Wait, I'll put the dog in another room.' He turned and led the dog away, then returned and invited Hennessey into the cottage. 'Cooler inside,' he said.

Hennessey swept off his panama and stepped gratefully into the cottage. He noted how thick the stone walls were and was intrigued by the date – 1670 – set in the wall above the fireplace.

'Cool in the summer, warm as toast in the winter, very easy to heat . . . and three hundred years old when the first man walked on the moon. Stephenson's the name. How can I help you?'

'I am calling in response to the incident five years ago. You may know of it?'

'Oh . . . yes . . . dreadful business.' Stephenson indicated a deep armchair. 'Please take a seat.' He sat in the other identical armchair, which stood at the far side of the hearth; both chairs were angled slightly away from each other. 'Bad business – heard more about it from the villagers than from the Percivals. They sold the cottage soon after – more or less immediately afterwards. Dare say they didn't feel safe here after that. I was mindful of the attack, which is why I laid the gravel and acquired Isaac, the dog. The gate always creaked; nothing like a creaking gate to deter a scoundrel.'

'Indeed.' Hennessey read the room. Comfortable: a man living within his means . . . not garish . . . just very, very homely. 'Did you know the Percivals?'

'No, never met. It was their weekend retreat. Cost me all my savings when I retired.'

'Her Majesty's forces?'

'Yes. Army. Lieutenant colonel. Never got the full colonelcy, but few achieve their goals. Lieutenant colonel is respectable enough and I had a damned interesting life. Well, they sold up lock, stock and barrel – everything was included. I mean everything – even the linen on the bed, and that was the only thing I changed. Threw out their linen, replaced it with new, but in all other respects the

21

cottage is as it was when the old fella was attacked. Found him lying here' – Stephenson pointed to the floor in front of him – 'at our feet. Had the carpet cleaned because it was stained with blood . . .'

'Very interesting . . . You see, this is why I visited: just to get a view of the crime scene, I had to visualize it.'

'Why? Are you investigating it again?'

'Not again. As we said to Mrs Percival, the case was never closed. A case is only closed following a conviction; but sadly Mr Percival died last week.'

'Oh . . . I am sorry . . . though I never knew him.'

'Yes . . . He was left with permanent brain damage, to which he eventually succumbed.'

'I see. So his death was directly linked to the injuries he sustained in the attack, which makes it murder – the old year-and-a-day rule having gone out the window.'

'Exactly.' Hennessey inclined his hat towards Stephenson. 'So it's a new murder investigation. We are taking a fresh look at the case with other personnel.'

'I see. Well, the house is a time capsule of what it was when the attack took place. The Percivals seemed to have just turned the key and walked away, instructing the estate agents to sell it as it was, all contents included. I found nothing of any value, but then it was only ever a weekend retreat. Nothing was disturbed upstairs, no sign of it being ransacked – the attackers wanted to harm the man. Rumour is, they left him for dead.'

'Seems that that was the case. Can I look outside?'

'Please . . .' Stephenson extended an open palm.

Hennessey stood and walked outdoors. He stood with his back to the cottage; Stephenson followed.

'Open ground,' Stephenson said, 'if that's what you are thinking.'

'I am.' Hennessey noted the large front garden, ending in a low hedge, a narrow grey road snaking between flat fields. No other buildings in the vicinity until the angular Norman tower of the church at Aldworth St Mary surrounded by the grey rooftops of the village about one mile distant. 'But the cottage isn't overlooked unless by a motor vehicle coming in this direction . . . and little room to park a car at the roadside.'

'Yes, car parking's at the rear of the cottage. They could have parked there, but I tend to think they didn't.'

'Oh . . .?'

'They would have come from over the fields.' Stephenson pointed to his left.

'Can you show me?'

'This way.' Stephenson led Hennessey away from the road to the far side of the cottage, where a small area of land, about ten feet wide, Hennessey judged, stood between the cottage and a high privet hedge. In the hedge a hole had been forced, and established as if by years of use. Beyond the hole was a meadow. 'You can just make out a pathway over the meadow – faint, but it's there.'

'Where does the pathway lead?'

'To the village. The path can't be seen from the house; there are no windows at either side of "Sundowner" cottage.'

'So, if Mr Percival was sitting in his cottage awaiting his wife's return, the first he would know of his attackers' presence was when they dashed past his cottage front window?'

'Yes.'

'They'd be in the cottage before he was out of his chair,' Hennessey mused.

'That's what I thought . . . and if they halted just here – this side of the cottage – they would be able to wait until they saw the lane was free of traffic, and no creaking gate to worry about. Probably waited here for hours – just waiting until the old boy was alone – then pounced.'

'Frightening thought.'

'Very.'

It was Monday, the second of June, 17.45 hours.

Two

Tuesday, 3 June, 09.00 hours – 14.00 hours
in which a crime scene is revisited, a slippery customer is engaged in conversation and a new link is discovered.

'Local knowledge,' Ventnor suggested. 'I mean, the blind spot beside the cottage, the hole in the privet fence, the route – can't really call it a path by your description, sir – the route back to the village. That's local knowledge, seems to me.'

'Good point.' Hennessey raised his eyebrows and also raised his index finger in Thompson Ventnor's direction.

'Other than that, we didn't get a great deal from Tommy White. Knew of the Saffers, dug their garden once when he worked for a landscape gardener – it's all in the file . . . but me – myself and Thompson – came away from Full Sutton with the impression we had just interviewed an innocent man.'

'Really?' Hennessey glanced at Yellich. 'You felt that? Both of you?'

'Somerled more than me, sir, but . . . well, let's just say that I wouldn't dismiss the possibility, having met him. Five years inside top-security and the really guilty felons start to look at the parole board, start to 'fess up; but not our boy. He's clinging to his not-guilty plea – clinging to his claim of innocence. The murder weapon was planted in his lock-up, as were the jewels stolen from the Saffers' house.'

25

Hennessey leaned forward and rested both elbows on his desk. 'We need to know more about Duncan Percival. Not a clean-living bloke by all accounts. He could easily have trodden on the wrong toes. We need to start asking questions; five years on, folk might be more willing to talk.' He paused. 'Anybody you really wanted to talk to five years ago, Ventnor? Someone you felt might be useful but wouldn't say anything?'

'Couple . . . more than two, in fact. All dodgy – seemed to have one foot in the legitimate business community and the other foot in organized crime, which is the environment that Percival seems to have inhabited.'

'Well, go and visit them again. Take Yellich with you.'

'Yes, boss.'

'Me – I'll go and visit the Saffers' relatives, their next of kin. Two elderly people, shot like that – I want to know more about them. I haven't got my finger on the pulse of that case.'

'You'll meet their son, boss.' Yellich stood. 'As I recall, he was moving into the house . . .'

'That's correct.' Ventnor also stood. 'I remember, too, he explained that the house had been in the family for generations – always occupied by the first-born male and his family. Not something I'd like to do – confess it is not.'

'Not something I'd like to do either,' Hennessey thought as he turned his car off the public road and into the drive of Milverton Hall. Like Apsley House, it had a vast lawn to the front, but Hennessey found it totally unlike Apsley House in all other respects. Milverton Hall occupied a position on the edge of a prosperous village and clearly had not had to sell off its grounds to a housing developer, since it stood in what Hennessey saw as being park-like acreage. The building itself seemed to be squat rather than tall. It plainly emanated from an original structure, with additional buildings added at later dates – not, he felt, added with particular sensitivity or architectural merit. The overall impression he had was that Milverton Hall was a hotch-potch of a building. Its red brick glowed in the sun, occasionally sending blue waves of convection current rising, shimmering from ground to eaves, giving the impression that the house was on fire.

Hennessey halted his car in front of the house, got out, walked up to the front door and pressed a modern-looking electric doorbell – the sort he was accustomed to seeing on the doorframes of much, much more modest houses, not at all the ancient bell pull or brass knocker he had been expecting. He pressed the bell twice but didn't hear a sound from within the building. He reasoned a house as cavernous as Milverton Hall would likely have the bell situated deep within the building and, in fairness, it would not be heard at the door. So he waited, turning as he did so to view the gardens: a closely mown lawn leading down to an ivy-covered stone wall and to the fields beyond the road, which ran behind the green wall. In a fleeting moment he likened ivy to snow: both delightful to behold, both very dangerous in their own way. To his right a small wood seemed to encompass a pond, which had a softening effect; to his left was another lawn, beyond which was dense shrubbery. He heard a bolt drawn across the door and turned to face the building.

'Yes . . . Can I help you?' The woman was dressed in a suit, had short-cropped silver hair, a slender build and a confident but not haughty manner. She was perhaps in her mid-fifties.

'Police.' Hennessey showed his ID.

'Ah . . . yes, do come in.' She stepped to one side, allowing Hennessey to enter the cool interior of the building. 'Thank you for your phone call; we did appreciate the warning. I am Mrs Saffer.'

'It also ensured that you would be at home' – Hennessey removed his hat – 'though courtesy was the overriding concern.'

'My husband is in his study . . . if you'd follow me, please.' Mrs Saffer led Hennessey from the vestibule to a door on the left, which she opened without knocking. 'The police, dear,' she said and then stepped back, inviting Hennessey to enter the room with a practised flourish of her wrist – open palm and extended fingers. Hennessey saw momentarily that she had exceptionally long fingers: an artist's hands, he thought. He entered the room as Mrs Saffer closed the door behind him.

'I am Paul Saffer.' The man stood and shook hands over his desk top. 'Please, take a pew.' He indicated a chair in front of his desk. He was of a similar age to his wife, with closely trimmed silver hair and an equally closely trimmed beard. He wore an open-necked blue shirt and white, light-weight trousers. 'How can I help you? You said it was about my parents' murder?'

'Yes . . . yes, it is.'

'I thought that was wrapped up: that unpleasant little creature White was convicted. My parents would have given him the jewellery; he didn't have to kill them. Both in their seventies, they had every right to expect to live their autumn years . . . a waste. Dare say the murder of someone in their twenties is more of a waste, but it's still a waste – still damned unfair. We have dogs – they're at the back; we let them out at night . . . four Dobermans . . . We bought them when we moved in.'

'You didn't live here at the time?'

'No, we lived in Malton, but upon my father's death I became the head of the family and we moved in. It's a very strange feeling, when your marital bed was the marital bed of your parents and grandparents and great-grandparents. Cleared out the cupboards . . . bought a new mattress and bedding . . . but it's a strange feeling.'

'I can imagine.'

'Well, that's what is expected of me. My great-grandfather bought this house, with the money he made from his ink-manufacturing company.'

'Saffer Inks? You are that family?'

'Yes, that's us. The market for bottled ink has shrunk. It's still there, though it is shrinking, at home especially, albeit exports to the developing world are still healthy. We have also moved with the times and are producing ink for the cartridges in computer printers.'

'I see.'

'But you are here about the murders?'

'Yes.'

'Why?' Saffer smiled. 'You are not going to tell me White is innocent?'

'Probably . . . We don't know yet. The possibility looms.'

'Oh, my . . .' Saffer sat back in the leather-upholstered chair. 'Well, I would not want the wrong person to be imprisoned.'

'Nor would we.'

'He helped dig the pond.' Saffer indicated behind him with a raised finger.

'Yes, I saw it . . . a pleasant feature.'

'It was my father's contribution to the house. The part we are in dates back to the seventeenth century. The extensions were added by my grandfather; no more extensions to be built, and so my father's contribution was to landscape the garden. It was like a large football pitch: dull, flat, uninteresting.'

Hennessey smiled, but a deep emotional pain gripped his chest.

'I well remember White in the landscape gardener's

29

crew – a cheery lad; it was a surprise to be told that it was he who had murdered my parents . . . and to see him in the dock . . . thinking him to have been a murderous animal all the while . . . despite his cheeriness . . . Now, perhaps . . .'

'Well, we hope to get to the truth.'

'Whatever I can do to help . . .'

'Well, tell me about the murder of your parents, from your perspective. Anything strike you – perhaps not then, but over the fullness of time?'

'Well, both then and, as you say, over the fullness of time, it seemed and still does seem a remarkably brutal murder for little reward – a handful of jewellery, grabbed on impulse. There were much more valuable items in the house than the items stolen, and just as easily spirited away.' Saffer grimaced. 'It was as if the motive was personal but made to look like a robbery gone badly wrong.'

'So who would be motivated to do such a thing?'

'Simon might have been so motivated. It didn't occur to me at the time, so this is the first time I have mentioned it.'

'Simon?' Hennessey reached into his jacket pocket for his notebook.

'Simon Saffer, my uncle – paternal uncle . . . He's an angry man.'

'Angry with your father?'

'Angry *at* him. Simon was disinherited by my grand-father for some reason . . . Totally left out of the will – not allowed any part of the business. He is burning with resentment and his attitude towards my father was . . . well, seemed to be bordering on hatred. Simon is quite capable of thinking along the lines of "If I can't have it, neither can you", but I never thought he'd carry that thinking to the point of multiple murder.'

'It's not unknown, Mr Saffer. I am shortly to retire. I

have been a police officer nearly all my working life and I have known people who have been murdered for less.'

'Yes . . . I occasionally read of such low murders in the newspaper.'

'So where would we find Simon Saffer?'

'I don't know his address. He moves much . . . but he's known to you. He's a lot younger than my father: he'll be in his sixties now.'

'Interesting . . . We'll go and have a chat with him. Does he live locally?'

'Yes: in and around York – mostly in, I believe . . . A bit of a drinker . . . Never seen him sober, though I have seen him only occasionally.'

'Well, if we know him, he won't be hard to find.'

'Can't see him doing it – getting hold of a shotgun, getting out here with a shotgun without anyone seeing him. Can't conceal a shotgun very easily. It wasn't as though it was a sawn-off; it was produced at White's trial.'

'Still easily concealed,' said Hennessey. 'They're all the same: break into three sections, butt, stock and barrel. Could be hidden in a golf-club bag or sports bag. Anyway, we'll have a little talk with him. Any other suspects?'

'Not that I can think of. Even Simon – Uncle Simon – that's pushing it a bit; but you never know.'

'Indeed,' Hennessey retorted; 'should there be anything else that occurs to you, please let us know, no matter how trivial it might seem.'

'Of course.' Saffer also stood. 'I'll see you to the door.'

'My husband's – my late husband's business contacts?' Margaret Percival seemed to Yellich and Ventnor to be perplexed by the question. 'Duncan mentioned little to me.'

'He never mentioned anybody? You never met anybody?' Yellich pressed.

'Well, if he had anything approaching a partner, or contact, it would have been Norman Broomfield.'

'Who is he?' asked Yellich.

'Where is he?' asked Ventnor.

'Who is he? I have just told you . . .' Margaret Percival stood square on to the two officers in the drawing room of thirty-two Hawksbridge Road. 'Where is he? I have to refer you to the phone book or the Yellow Pages, under Financial Services.'

Hennessey drove back into York, along a narrow road with a heavy volume of traffic, flat green fields on either side of the road, the occasional stand of trees, an isolated farmhouse – all baking under a relentless sun, all under a vast canopy of blue. He entered the sluggish traffic in York, swelled by tourists and day visitors, who enjoyed rides in open-topped double-decker buses or in horse-drawn carriages. He stop-started his way to Micklegate Police Station and, with no little sense of relief, parked his car in the 'Staff Only' car park at the rear of the building, leaving the driver's window wound down by a few inches to allow the car to breathe. He walked across the car park, grateful for his panama, as he felt the weight of the sun's heat upon his shoulders, and stepped into the welcoming cool of the police station. At his desk he recorded his visit to Paul Saffer of Milverton Hall in the growing file of the double murder of Julia and Julian Saffer, cross-referenced to the assault and subsequent murder of Duncan Percival as being 'possibly linked'. He phoned the collator and asked for any and all information on Simon Saffer, aged sixty plus, to be sent to him. He glanced at his watch . . . twelve ten p.m. It had perhaps been a useful morning – hardly a breakthrough, but the inquiry progressed, and now it was, he felt, time for lunch. He left his office on the CID corridor and walked slowly and calmly to the inquiry desk, where he signed out and, screwing his panama on to his head, walked out into the weight and glare of the sun.

He crossed the road and, as he did so, glanced up at the spikes on which heads of the beheaded had once been impaled, the most famous perhaps having been the head of Henry Percy, the eldest son of the Duke of Northumberland, who, by his practice of riding into the heat of battle, had earned himself the nickname of 'Harry Hotspur'. His head had remained impaled on the spikes of Micklegate Bar for three years, from 1403. Hennessey climbed the steps up on to the walls, which, despite being thronged with tourists, were still the speediest way to transit the city centre. To his right was the new building that had been erected on the site of the old, original railway station, the demolition of which seemed to have been done overnight before any voice of protest could be raised – a shame, in his view. The curved platform and the serrated roofline were still visible, clear examples of early nineteenth-century railway architecture. To his left, the roof of the new and present railway station, which, when it had been opened in 1877, had laid claim to being the longest in the world. He left the walls at the end of that section at Lendal Bridge, crossed over the Ouse, which was busy with trippers and a four-man scull pulling strongly with practised rhythm against the flow of the river. He turned right into Lendal and left into St Helen's Square, then entered the narrow, pedestrianized Stonegate, where street musicians and mime artists entertained for passing coins. He turned left and entered the cool of a snickelway whose narrowness led to the entrance of the Starre Inn, reputedly York's oldest pub. It was by then beginning to fill with lunch-time trade. Hennessey ordered a salad at the bar and a glass of lime and soda water and found a corner seat opposite a couple in their twenties, who clearly, he observed, had eyes only for each other. He envied their bliss and hoped it would long remain for them. While waiting for his meal to be brought to him, he pondered the framed print of an ancient map that hung on the wall adjacent to him, entitled 'The West Ridinge of Yorkshyre, with the moft famous and fayre Citie Yorke Defcribed', and dated 1610.

His meal taken gently, Hennessey left the Starre Inn and walked through the narrow streets, interweaving with the other foot-passengers, into Davygate and along Parliament Street,with its mix of ancient and modern. He turned left into Pavement, entered The Lady Peckett's Yard snickelway that provided not merely a short cut but a reprieve from the bustle, and thence into Fossgate. He followed Fossgate, crossing the canal-like litter-strewn River Foss at Walmgate, turned left into Hurst's Lane and thence into Percy's Lane. In Percy's Lane stood the Highwayman pub.

He entered the pub and turned left into the snug. It was empty save for one man, who beamed at Hennessey as he opened the door.

'Mr Hennessey!'

'Shored Up . . .' Hennessey returned the smile and walked across the warm carpet to the small hatch, which was the bar in the snug of the Highwayman, and rang the small handbell. When the barman, a round-faced man in his fifties with a ready smile and broad shoulders, appeared in the hatchway, Hennessey ordered a single Bells with Canadian dry ginger and a soda water and lime. He paid for the drinks and carried them both over to the table where the other man was sitting. He put the whisky in front of the man and sat opposite him. 'Your health' – he raised his glass.

'And yours, Mr Hennessey.' The man, short in stature,

with a gleam in his eye, raised his glass and sipped the whisky.

'Thought I might find you here, Shored Up.'

'Ah . . . here in the early afternoon is where I can drink in peace, and I am mightily pleased I ran into you, Mr Hennessey.'

'Oh?'

'Yes . . . I have a little problem.'

'Tell me – I am sure you will anyway.'

'Well, I was walking down the street and a constable – nice boy, well mannered, but oh, so determined – stopped me . . . asked to look inside the bag I was carrying.'

'Oh, he would. That's what comes of being known to the police, Shored Up.'

'Well, in the bag were a few trinkets – hardly anything really . . . This was the day before yesterday . . .'

'Don't tell me: charged with receiving stolen goods, released on bail?'

The man shrugged. 'What can I say?'

'So what was in the bag?'

'Some items of lady's wear.'

'You mean diamonds and gold – rings, bracelets and necklaces?'

'Of that ilk, Mr Hennessey, but I didn't know it was stolen – just looking after it for a friend.'

'Of course.' Hennessey nodded. 'And you don't know the name of your friend, do you?'

'I think he's called Terry; I see him at the Royal Oak occasionally.'

'So, somebody you see only occasionally entrusts you with a bag full of valuables? Come on, Shored Up, you know better than to try that. Try that with the magistrates and you'll bounce right back into the slammer.'

'Oh, I couldn't bear it' – the man's hand went to his head – 'all those rough boys.'

Hennessey squinted in response to the sun streaming into the pub through the frosted glass and illuminating specks of dust floating in the air. 'Yes, not quite what you were used to in the Officers' Mess of the Green Howards.'

'Devon and Dorsets, Mr Hennessey – I told you, I am sure I did. I decided I couldn't get away with masquerading as an ex-officer of a Yorkshire regiment: I might meet the real thing. So I thought the Devon and Dorsets would be safer. Still use the name Smythe, though – Colonel, at your service.'

'So who are you fleecing at the moment? Which little old, but very wealthy, lady is going to lose a fortune by sinking money into your family firm, which needs rescuing from the brink of bankruptcy, or your tin mine in Bolivia?'

'Couldn't tell you – won't tell you. You'll spoil it for me – phone her . . . tip her off.'

'Damn right I will. Do you know your jacket buttons are different from each other?'

'They are?' The man glanced down at his jacket buttons.

'Better get that seen to or your victim will know that Colonel Smythe (retired) draws his kit from the charity shops.'

'Ah . . . I owe you one, Mr Hennessey . . . but . . . but . . . I don't know – it adds to that air of genteel poverty, don't you think?'

'So what's the scam? Which one haven't you tried yet? Raising money to salvage a ship full of gold bullion?'

'Can't tell you that either, Mr H . . .' He tapped the side of his nose.

'So long as you know the consequences . . . Obtaining money by deception: five years.'

'The risk is the thrill, Mr Hennessey. You know, during the last sentence I served I used to escape the rough boys by joining the Christian Union. That's why we were all there – sitting in a circle round the chaplain, reading such and such a passage from verse something to verse something, or from verse something to the end. I always liked that phrase: 'verse twenty-two to the end'. Anyway, we were all there to escape the sports hall and the cells . . . gentle boys finding an escape; but one old chaplain used to go banging on about digging holes: if you dig a hole you'll fall into it.'

'The proverbs of Solomon, yes.'

'Well, he said that quite a lot: "You are all in a hole of your own making" – that's what he used to say; "and you can continue digging holes and then falling into them, or you can put your spade on one side – never pick it up again," or some such, which was a trifle unfair if the lag was genuinely innocent and also didn't allow for the lags who deliberately dug holes to fall into because they couldn't cope with life on the outside. But me – when he said that, I always used to think: "Well maybe you're right, but I have dug an awful lot of holes in my life and have managed to sidestep most of them." So I got collared for one scam in ten . . . It's like paying a form of tax: win some, lose some, but make sure you win more than you lose. That's how I see it.' He drained his glass, placed it on the table and pushed it towards Hennessey.

'Not yet. Don't have any illusions, Shored Up; we're watching you, especially now we know you are about to fleece someone. But I want information.'

'All I can give, Mr Hennessey, all I can give.'

'About five years ago a man called Percival – Duncan Percival – was attacked. You might remember: made a big splash in the local press?'

'Yes . . . in his weekend retreat, wasn't it? Little cottage in the Vale . . . left him for dead.'

'Yes, that's it. Well he died last week from his injuries – five

37

years after the attack . . . never anything but a vegetable in those five years, mind.'

'So now it's a murder inquiry?'

'Yes.'

'Don't think I can help you, Mr Hennessey. I have my ear to the ground, but I never did hear anything about that attack. Nobody talked. It was a professional job: not a whisper was heard; that was expensive labour, skilled labour. The only thing unskilled about it was that it was messy, for a job like that, where silence was kept, and kept for a long time afterwards. You'd expect a gun or a knife to have been used . . . but maybe not . . .'

'Well, it's not that I want to pick your brains, Shored Up . . .'

'No?'

'I want to know about the victim.'

'Ah . . .'

'Information we have received indicates that Mr Duncan Percival was . . . how shall I say . . .?'

'Bent.' Shored Up smiled. 'Try "bent", Mr Hennessey; he . . . now, he could teach me a thing or two. If only he had taken me under his wing I wouldn't have to hide in the Highwayman sponging free drinks off the law. You know the risk I take? If the wrong person sees me talking to the law – well, I'm finished . . . but the wrong people tend not to be daytime drinkers.'

'Very public-spirited of you,' Hennessey growled.

'No, it's not; I need favours doing, like charges being dropped . . . It's happened before . . . the present charge . . .'

'Just' – Hennessey held up his hand – 'just let us stay with what I want for the time being . . .'

Shored Up pushed his empty glass towards Hennessey.

'In a while . . . perhaps, depending on what information you can provide.'

Shored Up shrugged. 'What can I say? What can I tell you?'

'About Duncan Percival – you said he was bent. How bent?'

'So bent he looked straight – that bent. He dug holes as well – many holes; but unlike me he sidestepped every one . . .'

'Not every one: he was battered to death for a reason.'

'Dare say.'

'So who would want to do that? Whose toes did he step on?'

'Many and varied.'

'Names?'

'Well, you could try Toby Murphy, the used-car dealer.'

'Where do I find him and who is he?'

'In the Yellow Pages, but he used to be on the Tang Hall Estate. That fella lived in Nether Poppleton, big house. Then he was a 'Tangy', little council flat on the Tang Hall Estate, and it was Duncan Percival that put him there. He's bounced back now, but he lost everything once.'

'How?'

'Someone torched his business.'

'How?'

'Ask Murphy the details. You could ask a fella called Terry Wales; he's in his mid-forties; he has track for minor offences – drunk and disorderly . . . so his address will be known to you, but he has a gripe against Percival. You could also take a trip out to Full Sutton.'

'Why? Who's in there?'

'Many men . . .'

'Specifically?'

'Eddie Challis.'

'That name rings a bell.'

'He's doing life. He shot a guy.'

'Ralph Brodney – with a rifle . . . I remember.'

'Well, it wasn't intended that he got caught, but his wife and children are being well taken care of.' Again Shored Up tapped the side of his nose.

'You mean Duncan Percival was behind that murder?'

'Possibly, possibly not . . . but if you don't want to take a ride out to Full Sutton, you could talk to his victim's widow. In fact, that's probably a better idea.'

Hennessey took his notepad from his pocket and wrote the three names on a fresh page. 'Possibly I will.' He stood and, as he did so, he dropped a five-pound note on the table.

'About that charge, Mr Hennessey . . .?'

The house was low, sitting in a fold in the landscape; grey, remote, thought Yellich and Hennessey, though neither commented. It seemed to Yellich that it had once been a farmhouse but was now encased in a low brick wall that shut it off from the surrounding land. It was accessed by a drive along a pitted road about a quarter of a mile in length. As he believed befitted country living, Yellich sounded the horn as he drove along the road towards the house. Hennessey glanced at him questioningly.

'Never come up on someone in the country,' he said; 'learned that lesson a long time ago. Country folk can react violently if you creep up on them; they have a bigger sense of space than city dwellers; they appreciate a warning.' He pressed the horn again. A curtain in the house was pulled back and then was let fall again. 'Our presence is announced.'

'Seems so,' Hennessey growled.

'This guy is not a suspect.' Yellich slowed the car as they approached the house. 'Not yet anyway. We might need his cooperation; don't want to get off on the wrong foot.'

'We don't want to pussyfoot around, either. We are the

police; they are not.' Hennessey glanced to his left. 'But you're right about warning people in the country as you approach them. I'll remember that.'

The door of the house opened. A bearded man, wearing a baggy, long-sleeved shirt and shorts, stood in the doorway. He raised his hand – not so much in greeting as to shield his eyes from the sun as he watched the car approach. Yellich halted the car in front of the house and he and Hennessey got out.

'Can I help you?' The bearded man's voice contained a note of caution, of wariness.

'Hope so.' Hennessey smiled. 'Police.' He showed his ID.

'Ah . . .' The bearded man smiled. He was clearly relieved.

'We'd like to ask you a couple of questions.'

'Only a couple? Long drive out from York for just two questions. Presume you're come from York?'

'Yes. Micklegate Bar.'

'Ah . . . I've been in the cells there a few times. Care to come in? The sun's fierce – too fierce for me. I don't do well in the heat.' He turned his back on Yellich and Hennessey and walked into the house.

The house was, Yellich found, untidy, though not unclean, and smelled strongly of turpentine and oil paint.

'Please' – the bearded man extended his right arm with palm upturned – 'please, take a pew . . . any pew, they're all the same.'

'You are Mr Simon Saffer?' Yellich asked as he sat in a comfortable-looking armchair.

'I am, and I didn't do it.' Saffer sat. 'Whatever it is you are investigating, I didn't do it. I don't drink any more.'

'We know . . . At least we assumed that. No convictions for ten years.'

'Yes . . . The bottle seems to hold the answer at times but only seems to – just makes things go away for a while.

You wake up with a hangover and things haven't changed. So, how can I help you?'

'We are here in connection with the murder of your brother Julian and his wife Julia Saffer.'

'Why?' Simon's draw dropped. 'That is all wrapped up, isn't it? A farm worker, Tommy White, is doing life.'

'Yes, we know.' Yellich spoke softly.

'It's perhaps not as wrapped up as it seems,' Hennessey added.

'Oh . . .?'

'Yes, we are taking another look at the case.'

'The case? That was my brother.'

'Sorry, that was insensitive.' Yellich nodded in response to Simon Saffer's complaint. 'We have visited your nephew, Mr Paul Saffer, at Milverton Hall.'

Simon Saffer groaned. 'He will have painted a dark picture of me, no doubt.'

'We understand that you were disinherited?' Yellich asked.

'We didn't know that at the time,' Hennessey explained.

'Am I a suspect?'

'Well' – Yellich shifted in his chair – 'we are looking again at the case, a fresh look, so on that basis then, yes, you are under suspicion if only because everybody is under suspicion.'

Simon Saffer settled back. 'That is very interesting. So the man I have been dismissing as a spineless little nothing might be innocent after all?'

'Yes . . . he might.'

'Well, what a turn-up for the books.'

'How did you feel about being disinherited, Mr Saffer?'

'Ah . . .' Saffer smiled. 'So that's what you think: a Cain-and-Abel number. I was disinherited so I blew my own brother away out of resentment?'

'Did you?'

'No. I didn't have – dare say I still don't have – an alibi for that day . . . but I don't need one.'

'You don't?'

'No, I don't have to prove my innocence; you have to prove my guilt. But, no – I didn't murder my brother. Dare say that's something Paul told you or put into your mind. That's the Saffer family . . . backstabbing. It never was a united family; internecine, in a word . . . but more subtle than murder. Destroy, yet not commit a crime in the process . . . blackening each others' names, betraying each other. I thought at the time that the person who invented the family should be shot; subsequently changed my mind on that point.'

'Can we ask why you were disinherited, Mr Saffer?'

'I married out.'

'Married out?'

'Of my race . . . I committed the unforgivable sin of marrying an Asian lady and bringing a black woman into the family was enough for my father to banish me with bell, book and candle . . . excommunicated . . . outlawed . . . for life. It was the last straw; I wasn't interested in becoming part of the family business – that exasperated the old boy, but I pointed out that if my heart wasn't in it, it was best for all that I was well out of it. Confess I did drink a little . . . Wasn't expecting to be cut off without a penny. After growing up in Milverton Hall and enjoying a very privileged education, it was a bit of a shock to find myself renting a small room in a shared house in Holgate . . . just me and my wife, Anveri. She was a Muslim and didn't understand the lure of alcohol.'

'Was?'

'She is deceased. Gave me two lovely children of the male sex, lived to see them both start and one complete their university studies . . .'

'I am sorry.' Yellich spoke softly.

'Thanks, but I have made the adjustment and my work is a source of comfort. I am an artist . . . a painter. I felt the ghost in me to paint from an early age, and I just could not be a businessman. I might have kept some inheritance but "marrying out", as my father put it, was the end. So, to answer your question, sir, as to how I felt about being disinherited: the answer is that I felt proud. I was, still am, very proud of my late wife, and am very proud of my two sons. Both are now university teachers . . . and I am proud that my life is not sullied by the Saffer money. I wouldn't want it on those terms. It would be immoral money.'

Yellich smiled and thought, Good for you. He asked, 'If Tommy White didn't murder your brother and his wife, do you know who might have a motive for doing so?'

Saffer opened his palms in a gesture of despair. 'He was a businessman . . . he made enemies . . . but he wasn't a local businessman. Saffer Ink is distributed globally. He didn't upset local people. If someone had a grudge against him, they would have travelled from overseas to murder him and my sister-in-law. Yet the person who did murder them knew little Tommy White and his lock-up. That's local knowledge; doesn't add up and deliver, to my mind; but then that's your department, as they say.'

'Doesn't, does it?' Yellich murmured.

'Doesn't add up at all,' Hennessey added. 'International businessman and wife murdered by someone with local knowledge.'

Saffer smiled. 'Perhaps it was that all along: a clumsy burglary that went badly awry . . . and possibly Tommy White really is the guilty party. But it's up to you to find out. What has caused the case to be reopened, may I ask?'

'Yes . . . a serious assault – a totally unrelated case which has just become murder. The person died from his injuries. Took five years, but that means it is a murder case, and your brother and sister-in-law's murder seems to be related somehow.'

'Who was murdered?'

'Gentleman by the name of Duncan Percival; do you know of him?'

'I'll say!'

'Really?' Yellich stiffened, as did Hennessey.

'Yes. He is as local and as uncouth a character as you could not want to meet. He wasn't a business rival but he and my brother quarrelled. Percival built on his land.'

'He built on his land!'

'Yes. Would you credit it? That's Percival for you: so arrogant we . . . wondered about his sanity. He had land which abutted land my brother owned, and the building he put up crossed the boundary – not by a matter of inches but by quite a substantial amount . . . measured in many hundreds of square feet.'

'So being disinherited didn't stop you sharing in your family's business?'

'I was kept informed; my brother would chat to me; he would call in and jaw. He was a lot older than me and I think he felt protective of me. Gave me money from time to time . . . told me about Percival. My brother did the dirty on Percival . . .'

'Oh?'

'Yes, he didn't obtain an injunction to stop him building, which would have cut Percival's losses. He waited until the building was complete, pretended he was unaware of it going up, then went to court, civil action, obtained a court order to have it demolished . . . the whole lot. He sat where you are sitting and said, "I could stop him now, but he needs to be taught a lesson and so I'll wait until it's finished; that will cost him deep in the purse."'

'Hmm . . . we thought the two cases were connected. That might just be it . . . except that your brother and his wife were murdered after Percival was attacked; he was in a coma by then,' Hennessey mused.

'Well, he could have dispatched his dogs of war, unable to recall them. The incident of his building on our land was just before my brother was murdered – a few months, as I recall. But again, that's your department.'

It was Tuesday, the third of June, 14.00 hours.

Three

Tuesday, 3 June, 14.45 hours – 22.30 hours
in which a Border collie points to a dead man and Inspector
George Hennessey is at home to the gentle reader.

She was a lady in mourning, though gracefully so: black-lace dress, black gloves, black nylons, black shoes and doubtless, thought Yellich, a black hat and black veil when she went out of doors. Mrs Margaret Percival received Yellich and Ventnor in the drawing room of Apsley House. 'I felt I should observe a period of mourning,' she explained.

'Of course,' Yellich replied.

'It seemed only fitting. My dear husband was deceased to all intents and purposes five years ago – when that thug, or thugs, left him for dead. Poor Duncan, but in a sense I am pleased for him – a persistent vegetative state is no quality of life.'

'Yes.' Yellich nodded. 'I would have to agree with you.'

'But his life had to run its course.'

'Again, yes.'

'I shall be mourning for approximately one month . . . until the first of July; that appears seemly.'

'A matter for you, Mrs Percival.'

'The funeral will be stressful, I fear, very stressful.'

'Oh?'

'Yes, there will be Mrs Tennock there . . . and myself and the priest . . . we three.'

'Mrs Tennock?'

'Or Nurse Tennock. She attended Duncan daily, seven days a week, save for the holidays she negotiated. A dear . . . She lives further down Hawkridge Road – number seventy-six, I believe. So there will be just we three. I am due to visit the parish priest at the vicarage tomorrow to discuss the service. I hope he does not insist on a hymn. Oh . . . think . . . three of us struggling through a hymn in a church. Oh, but anyway, that is for me to deal with. So, how may I help you, gentlemen?'

'Well, I understand your husband had a run-in with the Saffer family?'

'He had many run-ins with many people. He was a businessman, it goes with the territory; and he kept me well separate from his business.'

Yellich glanced out of the windows of the drawing room – two huge sheets of glass, twelve feet high, four feet wide – out across a closely cut lawn to the garden wall and the red-tiled roof of the newbuild houses that surrounded the grounds of thirty-two Hawkridge Road and the vast, cloudless blue sky above. 'This you may have heard of. It was a dispute over a building that was built on Saffer-owned land. Saffer knew the building was going up but didn't raise an objection until it was complete, then successfully sued for the building to be demolished.'

'Yes.' Mrs Percival smiled. She was slender, with chiselled features – very attractive in a middle-aged way, thought Yellich, very poised, very restrained, very lady-of-the-manor, very likely to acquire a new significant other in her life, very easily and speedily.

'You do recall that issue?'

'Yes, that I do. I wasn't part of it, of course, just not allowed: my place was here, not in the office; but I do remember his thundering about it and I read it in the newspaper – it received a short mention. It cost my husband a lot of money. Over a million pounds, I believe.'

'As much as that?'

'Yes, it was a . . . well, it was going to be a privately owned hall of residence for university students . . . a nice little earner. He thought he'd be into profit within twenty years. It was going to be his retirement income, his pension. In the end, not only did he have to pay for the thing to be built, he had to pay for it to be pulled down, demolished, and the bricks taken away and the site restored to nature. Then he got a massive legal bill from his solicitor. He hired a very expensive barrister but the case was a loser from the outset. Saffer claimed he hadn't known the building was going up until it was completed. Duncan's QC argued that he had known very well it was being built but had very cruelly and spitefully waited until it was completed before he took out an injunction to have it demolished, knowing that Duncan would, by then, have paid the contractors for the building. Saffer pointed out that the building was on a greenfield site on the other side of York, which he intended to keep as a greenfield site as his contribution to the environment, and so he'd had no reason ever to visit it. He said it was a shock to see that it had been built on, and that' – Margaret Percival held up a long finger – 'and that is half truth, apparently. It wasn't wholly built on Saffer's land; it did overlap . . . or encroach upon it by about a few hundred square feet.' She lowered her hand, keeping her restrained and, in Yellich's eyes, somewhat regal poise. 'I am not . . . was not, privy to the details, but I understand my husband's two very reasonable offers were rejected by Saffer.'

'What were they? Do you know?' Ventnor leaned forward in his chair.

'Yes; I believe the first offer was that my husband should purchase the land he had inadvertently built on.'

'Fair enough.'

'Saffer refused, even though the offer was, I believe, substantially more than the land was worth . . . and the other solution proposed by my husband was that he should purchase a parcel of land which was on the other side of Saffer's greenfield site, which was greater than the area he had built on, in exchange for the title to the disputed land.'

'Again' – Ventnor nodded – 'seems fair and reasonable.'

'So I would have thought, but Saffer refused; very pig-headed of him . . . Anyway, the upshot was that the building was demolished – a great loss to my husband. He has left me comfortably off, but I'd be a million pounds better off without that incident – more than a million pounds better off, because I would be deriving an income from the halls of residence . . . five hundred students paying me rent. Very handsome.'

'Five hundred?'

'Yes, it was a huge building, like a block of flats. It's incomprehensible that Saffer didn't know it was partly on his land . . . but that's history.'

'So your husband had some motive to want to harm Saffer?'

'Oh yes.' Margaret Percival's jaw set firm. 'He ranted and raved about what he'd like to do to Saffer . . . but someone got to Duncan . . . got to Duncan first. I have often wondered . . . no . . . I won't . . . I won't be cynical.'

'If you have your suspicions, Mrs Percival . . .' Yellich probed gently.

'Well, my husband was well known in the business community and known to be violent . . . if not violent in himself, then capable of orchestrating violence. It would have reached Saffer's ears that my husband was seeking the sweetness of revenge and so I have wondered whether or not the Saffer family organized a pre-emptive strike. York is a graceful city – its ancient buildings, its museums, its higgledy-piggledy streets, and everything else that the tourists come to see: the elegant Minster . . . more ghosts than any other city . . . including the most frequently seen ghost in the UK, averaging two appearances a year, I believe; but . . . there is an unpleasant underbelly to the famous and fair: it can be a very violent place. It has its gangland, its organized crime. There is muscle for hire in York if you know where to seek it and have the means to pay for it.'

'And you think Saffer hired protection and someone to attack your husband?'

'Well, I would, if I thought my very angry husband was out to kill me because I had caused him to lose a million pounds, then yes . . . I'd start asking questions . . . looking for someone who could put me in touch with someone, who could put me in touch with someone who could take care of my problem for a bag full of hard cash and no questions asked. Wouldn't you?'

'No, I wouldn't,' Yellich replied.

'But then, we're the law,' Ventnor added. 'Well, thank you; it's been useful. We'll see ourselves out.'

Margaret Percival smiled.

Outside the house, where a pale youth was washing a blood-red Ferrari, Yellich and Ventnor walked towards Yellich's car and then paused as a canary-yellow soft-top BMW turned from Hawkridge Road into the drive of Apsley House. It purred towards the building and drove to the stables at the side of the house. The muscular man at the wheel – dark-haired, conventionally handsome, about thirty years of age, so thought both Ventnor and Yellich – glanced at Yellich and Ventnor dismissively as he and the car disappeared from view.

Yellich glanced at Ventnor. 'Milady has comfort in her mourning, methinks.'

'Methinks you are correct.' Ventnor smiled. 'Methinks.'

*　　*　　*

Having completed his conversation at the Highwayman pub, George Hennessey returned to Micklegate Bar Police Station, wearing a casual panama atop his head, light-weight jacket over his forearm, pushing through the crowds of tourists being entertained by street performers – here a duo of violinists, there a rough-looking youth with a tin whistle (who, Hennessey thought, must have only just scraped a pass mark in his street entertainers' test in order to obtain his licence); here a gaily clothed juggler, there a man with silver flesh paint in Victorian costume, standing motionless, statue-like, arms bent in front of him, and many others. York, mid-afternoon, the height of summer.

Hennessey chose to walk up Micklegate rather than take the usual and more efficient route along the walls, reasoning that narrow Micklegate would afford more shade than would the exposed battlements. At the top of Micklegate he crossed Nunnery Lane and entered the cool of the police station. He signed in and checked his pigeonhole, noting only routine circulars. He entered the CID corridor and walked slowly to his office, noting as he did so that both Yellich and Ventnor were still out. He was pleased to note that they seemed to be working well together, reinforcing his impression that Ventnor, an unknown quantity, would prove an asset.

He hung his jacket on the back of his chair and on a moment's impulse, knowing he was not being observed, skimmed his hat through the air to the hatstand. It missed – not greatly, to his surprise, but he still felt a pang of disappointment as it fell gracelessly on to the floor, having first impacted with the wall. He strode forward, knelt and picked it up, and placed it carefully on a peg. He took the file on the murder of Duncan Percival and wrote up his interview with Paul Saffer, drawing attention to the powerful motivation that Duncan Percival had for murdering Saffer's parents or, more likely, having them murdered, the arrangements for which could so easily have been put in motion and made before he himself had been bludgeoned in his weekend retreat. He also recorded his chat with Shored Up, who had told him of Toby Murphy, the used-car dealer who had been ruined by Duncan Percival; of Terry Wales, an associate of his with a history of minor offences; of Eddie Challis, presently in gaol for murder, again believed to have been acting on behalf of Duncan Percival; and of Mrs Ralph Brodney, widowed as a consequence – all to be visited. Unusually for a police officer, Hennessey did not like driving, though his reason was highly personal and deeply felt; but there were times when he couldn't avoid getting behind the wheel, and this, he reasoned, was one such. He collected his hat and jacket, walked back to the enquiry desk and signed himself out to HM Prison, Full Sutton.

'Depends whether this is on or off the record.' Eddie Challis reminded Hennessey of a weasel: glinting steel-blue eyes, quick, hurried movements, a false smile, carroty ginger hair. Challis was short in terms of stature, but lithe and muscular, probably well able to bench-press more than twice his body weight. A tough little hard man who, like Shored Up, saw prison as a form of taxation: get away with nine, get done for the tenth – fair's fair. He snatched at the cigarette that Hennessey offered and held it as Hennessey extended the lighter.

He had been shown into the agent's room with its two-tone paint, cream above red, with an opaque glass window set high in the wall, and waited as Edward 'Eddie' Challis, had been brought from the cells. He'd appeared eventu-ally among the sound of a juggling of keys, dressed in a blue striped shirt and jeans and soft trainer shoes, also blue. Hennessey had invited him to sit opposite him, produced the packet of cigarettes and said he wanted to talk about Duncan Percival.

Hennessey inclined his head to one side. 'Off the record, if you'd prefer. See where it leads . . . until it has to go on the record.'

Challis leered at Hennessey. 'You cops, you're like a barrowload of monkeys: say one thing, mean another.' He drew heavily, thankfully, on the cigarette.

'It's only on the record if it's written down and you sign it. You don't see a statement form in front of me, do you?'

'OK.'

'So, Percival, Duncan Percival – what do you know about him?'

'Some things . . . not enough. He's the reason I'm in here.'

'So I believe.'

'I did a job for him.'

'Shot someone?'

'Yes . . .'

'And other jobs for him?'

'Possibly . . . but that's not even off the record.'

'Very well. You shot a gentleman called Brodney?'

'Yes . . . Life with a minimum of twenty years. The army taught me to shoot, had to do something when I was time-expired, so I went to work for Percival.'

'As?'

'As . . . I was one of his persuaders.'

'Persuaders?'

'Yes . . .' Challis took another deep drag on the cigarette and exhaled down his nose. 'See, if some bloke didn't see things Percival's way, he'd send me and a couple of others round to see him, help the bloke see things Percival's way. Didn't take much doing.'

'I'll bet it didn't.'

'Well that was the only trade the army taught me . . . Not my fault, and I've got to make a living.'

'So why did you shoot Ralph Brodney?'

'Because I was hired to.'

'By Percival?'

'Yes. Twenty thousand pounds he paid me, over and above my weekly wage.'

'Cheap, really . . .'

'You think?'

'Well, it works out at a thousand pounds a year.'

'Yeah, well, I wasn't supposed to get caught, was I? That wasn't part of the script.'

Hennessey reeled from Challis's halitosis; the man clearly had advanced gum disease and the hum from his body indicated to Hennessey that Challis's weekly trip to the showers was imminent.

'If I hadn't been arrested, it would have been a nice little earner.'

'So, where is the money?'

'In a shoe box.'

'Meaning a bank account?'

Challis shrugged. 'Let's just say it's safe, along with all the other dosh I had. I've got it to come out to.'

'So Percival paid you to murder Mr Brodney?'

'Yes. He denied it . . . that's Percival: he never gets anywhere near the action, pays in hard cash, used notes, half up front, the rest on completion. Always uses a gofer. I never met him but once. After I was recruited I never saw him, just waited at home until the phone rang. The gofer would tell me where to go, where to pick up the money, who to visit . . . Nice work, easy money' – he smiled – 'and there's a little bonus to come out to.'

'Oh yes?'

'A bit of dosh if I keep my mouth shut and more work for Mr Percival when I get out.'

'That kind of confession could seriously harm your parole chances.'

'What confession? It's off the record.'

'Whatever – but do you think Percival will employ you after you grassed him up?'

'I didn't. It was the gofer that squealed. He drove me to Brodney's house, drove me away. Witness saw the car, gave a description; the house was remote. Before you knew it, the police helicopter was shining its little light all over us; had us cold, no point in continuing in the car, so I told the gofer to let me off, I was going to leg it. The gofer thought it was a good idea, so he stopped the car; he went one way, I went the other . . . The helicopter could only track one of us, and it followed Mule.'

'Mule?'

'The gofer – he was called Mule: Mule Mulligan. Irish name, but he comes from Manchester. Well, you know the rest . . .'

'Tell me . . . remind me.'

'Well, I got away, clean away. Mule, the gofer – he did well. He ran where the cars couldn't follow, meant the helicopter had to stay with him. He was a fit bloke – probably still is – kept the helicopter on him for two hours. I reached a road, found a bus shelter, rested there and then . . .'

'A bus came along?'

'Yes. So I was back in York before last orders were called. I needed *that* drink, I can tell you. Think of it: supping pint after pint in the snug of the Salutation, a bag over my shoulder with the gun inside.'

'Brave of you, Eddie.'

'Or plain stupid . . . but I needed that drink. The first one went down without touching the sides. Walked home and tossed the gun into the river. Mule and me, we swore we wouldn't grass, so I slept that night – just earned twenty thousand smackers for an hour's work.' Challis shrugged and stubbed the butt of the cigarette in the ashtray. 'Mule – he'd never been inside . . . you guys put the screw on him . . .'

'As we would.'

'Told him he was looking at life for conspiracy to murder . . . the big M . . . He folded, he didn't have any bottle . . . probably still doesn't. He's a marked man; he should have done the life, smiled nicely at the chaplain, and kept his trap shut. He wouldn't have done more than ten years, probably less . . . but he hadn't got the backbone to do that, so he squealed, turned Queen's evidence and grassed me and Percival . . . and told all he could tell about Percival. Went into witness protection – new name, new identity; but he can't hide for ever. One day he'll be outed. Then he's a dead man. He stood up in the box at the High Court and fingered me for the murder, but Duncan Percival is too fly . . . What Mule said during my trial was probably nothing to the amount of information he gave to the police – you guys – about Percival. But I'm keeping my mouth shut. I'm no grass.'

'Percival's dead.'

Eddie Challis's jaw dropped, his face drained of colour.

'Few days ago,' Hennessey continued.

'You're not kidding?' Challis held eye contact with Hennessey.

'Nope.'

'I heard he was done over . . . he was given a kicking . . . Seemed quiet after that.'

'He was alive but in name only. Persistent vegetative state.'

Eddie Challis gasped. 'I didn't know that.'

'Eventually died from his injuries a few days ago, so we are treating it as murder.'

Challis remained silent.

'So . . .' – Hennessey offered Challis another cigarette – 'so you have no reward to come out to . . . and no employment either.' He flicked the lighter and held the flame so that Challis could light the cigarette. 'Time to start helping yourself, Eddie. There's nobody out there doing you favours and there hasn't been anybody out there for you for the last five years.'

'You think?' Challis smiled.

'Who?'

'Mrs Percival.'

'She knew nothing of Duncan Percival's business dealings.'

'Oh yeah.' Challis pulled hard on the cigarette and again exhaled through his nose. 'I suppose she said that . . .'

'Yes.'

'And you believed her.' Challis smirked. 'You're not a new copper, you must be close to retirement; you are too old to be naive, Mr Hennessey.'

'Keep talking.'

'The Percivals were a real Bonnie-and-Clyde outfit. He was in the driving seat but she was the front-seat passenger . . . even holding the road map – that was my impression; but then, I was rarely in their house, Apsley House. Most times I was phoned up and Mule Mulligan called for me when there was some persuading to be done and someone needed cooling, like Ralph Brodney.'

'Why was Brodney murdered?'

Challis shrugged, 'Mine not to reason why' – he pulled on the cigarette – 'but it was business.'

'Business?' Hennessey asked.

'Not personal. Brodney was like Percival: two blaggers. Brodney was getting in the way of Percival; it was a turf-war thing.'

'I see. So who would be able to tell me about Mrs Percival?'

'Mule . . . ask Mule, or whatever his name is now. He lived in the house, in a little room, right at the back. He was their gofer twenty-four/seven . . . a real "steppan fetchit".'

'Very interesting.'

'But that didn't come from me.'

'Of course. Does the name Saffer mean anything to you?'

'The ink-makers?'

'Yes. We understand that Duncan Percival and the Saffers had a run-in over a building.'

'A building?'

'Percival built a house partly on land owned by the Saffer family and had to demolish it.'

Challis grinned. 'Was that the reason it was pulled down? He wouldn't be a happy camper about that . . . neither would she . . . but they wouldn't touch Saffer.'

'You think not.'

Challis shook his head. 'Quality people – on the right side of the law – and Percival was shrewd: only do something if there is something to be gained. I remember reading about the old couple being murdered, the Saffer murders, and the guy that was convicted of it, Tommy White; he's on the same wing as me. Good lad. If you're looking at Percival for that, forget it. Yes, he was angry with them, but he hadn't anything to gain from murdering them.'

'They cost him over a million pounds.'

'That's no reason to murder someone. The money is still lost, isn't it?' Challis inclined his head and smiled. 'That's the way Percival would have thought. He could stand that loss . . . and more . . . and a shotgun . . . messy. Nobody that Percival employed would use a shotgun; they'd use a point two-two, like me . . . close-up headshot . . . guaranteed success . . . fairly quiet too.'

'This has been good; more cooperation like this and you'll be working towards your parole.'

'Naw . . .' Challis shook his head. 'I'll shave a little time by good behaviour, but not by giving information. I want to work for Mrs Percival when I get out.'

Hennessey drove back to York, an hour's uneventful drive across the summer-lush Vale of York, a drive that a person who enjoyed motoring would have savoured. At Micklegate Bar he found that Yellich and Ventnor had returned from visiting Margaret Percival.

'Not as black as he's painted, then, is he, our Simon Saffer' – Yellich rested his elbows on his knees, leaning forward to speak – 'even allowing for a bit of PR on his part.'

'Seems to have been a bit wild in his younger days but is settled now and not bothered about being disinherited,' Ventnor added.

'Yes, and with him and his brother remaining on good terms,' Hennessey advised, 'there's no motivation to kill him . . . but someone who would have motivation was – would you believe – Duncan Percival.'

Yellich and Ventnor then filled him in on their last chat with Margaret Percival.

'So, Saffer claimed not to have known the building was being built . . .' Hennessey began.

'He was untruthful there,' Yellich added.

'So, Simon Saffer told us that his brother visited him and told him about the building. He said he was going to wait until it was complete and then force its demolition. What did he say?' Yellich turned to Hennessey. 'Cost him – something?'

'"Deep in the purse".'

'That was it. Julian Saffer told his brother that Percival needed to be taught a lesson or something.'

'"Needs a lesson learning",' Hennessey quoted.

'That was it: he was going to wait until the building was up, and then force it to be demolished, so it would cost Percival deep in the purse because he needed a lesson learning.'

'Some motivation there, you might think,' Ventnor suggested.

'You might indeed, except I visited Full Sutton, spoke to Eddie Challis – he's doing life for murdering another crim at Percival's behest; he described himself as one of Percival's "persuaders". Anyway, Challis says the attack on the Saffers was too messy to have been ordered by Percival, and that Percival would have stood the loss.'

'A million pounds – he could stand that loss?'

'Seems so. Challis claims Percival wouldn't do anything without a purpose.'

'Revenge is a purpose, sir,' Ventnor appealed. 'A million-pound loss!'

'Possibly, but the really interesting thing that came out of my visit to Full Sutton and my chat with Challis is that Mrs Percival is no angel.'

'No?'

'No, not according to Challis – described them as a "Bonnie-and-Clyde" pair.'

'Well, well, well . . .'

'I still think these two murders are related. I now want to find out more about Margaret Percival.'

'Lean on her, boss?' Yellich suggested.

'No. She's not in the frame for anything . . . yet. I'm going to visit the man who turned Queen's evidence against Eddie Challis; he's in witness protection. I'll find out who his handler is and then visit him. Write your visit up in the file, as I will mine. Then you two go and call on Mrs Brodney.'

'Who's she, boss?'

'The widow of one Ralph Brodney, shot by Eddie Challis on the orders of Duncan Percival. Dig out the file and find her address. Anything she can tell us about the Percivals, particularly Mrs.'

'Got it, boss.' Yellich stood, as did Ventnor.

Charlotte Pacey saw the man. She was walking her dog in Plantation Wood, as she often did, as near daily as she could. A drive out to the wood, then into the shade of the foliage, because her dog, a Border collie, like all dark dogs, suffered in the heat. On that day the walk was as any other: no person about, just her and Jack – until about ten minutes into the walk, when the dog stopped and pointed. Each dog, as Charlotte Pacey knew, has its own distinct way of pointing and her collie would point by standing still, head slightly lowered and looking directly at what he was pointing at. Charlotte Pacey walked up to her dog, patted him and followed his stare. She saw the man quite clearly but thought she would probably not have noticed him had not the dog pointed. She approached him cautiously, though intuitively she knew he was dead. She stopped when she was within ten feet of the body. The young man was clothed appropriately for his age – jeans, T-shirt, jogging shoes, no wristwatch or other items of male jewellery – lying there on the bed of bluebell leaves. No injury that Charlotte Pacey could see, but dead; no sign of the chest moving, even in the slightest – and the pallor. Charlotte Pacey had been a nurse for many, many years, had specialized in terminal care and knew death when she saw it. She turned away from the body, plunged her hand into her jacket pocket and extracted her mobile phone. She dialled three nines.

'Short walk for you today, Jack, me boy,' she said as she and the collie made their way back to her car to await the blues and twos.

*　　*　　*

Hennessey arrived at the scene, parking his car behind the black, windowless mortuary van, inside which the driver and his mate sat reading tabloid newspapers and smoking cigarettes. For them it was just another body to be lifted and conveyed to York District Hospital, Department of Pathology. Hennessey walked past the mortuary van and the line of police vehicles and took the path that led from the road to the wood, and to the blue-and-white police cordon within the wood, containing an inflatable tent with a police constable standing at the entrance. Hennessey saw Yellich chatting to a white-shirted sergeant. Behind them a line of constables was sweeping the wood.

'Afternoon, sir.' Yellich nodded as Hennessey approached.

'Sergeant.' Hennessey brushed a fly away from his face.

'Plenty more of those inside the tent, sir.'

'I imagine. What have we got?'

'Deceased of the male sex, sir, gunshot wound to the side of the head. Dr Mann, the police surgeon, pronounced life extinct just fifteen or twenty minutes ago, sir.' Yellich consulted his notepad. 'At sixteen forty-five hours, in fact.'

'Shot, you say?'

'Yes, sir, according to the police surgeon. Well, he identified two bullet holes in the side of the head; whether that was the cause of death is, of course, still to be determined. I have requested the pathologist's attendance.'

'Good.' Hennessey glanced at the tent and brushed another fly from his face. 'Just when we were gathering pace with the Saffer–Percival inquiry, this happens. But this is fresh. The Saffer–Percival murders are five years old; they can wait a while yet; dare say they'll have to.' He walked to the tent and the constable stepped aside to allow him ingress. He opened the tent flap and viewed the corpse: a young man, a boy, lying as if asleep, though he noticed the pallor observed by Charlotte Pacey, while the flies – a buzzing, dancing mass of the beasts – darting excitedly over their prize, told their own story. He stepped back out of the tent, grateful to be able to enjoy more breathable air and, as he did so, saw a red-and-white Riley RMA halt behind his own car. He felt a glow of warmth in his chest. He walked back to where Yellich and the uniformed sergeant stood.

Dr D'Acre left her car, exiting the vehicle gracefully, swivelling on her bottom, keeping both knees and ankles together. She wore green coveralls, carried a black Gladstone bag and walked towards the officers in a confident, upright manner. 'Good afternoon, gentlemen,' she said warmly when she was comfortably within earshot.

'Ma'am,' Hennessey, Yellich and the uniformed sergeant replied in unison.

'I was hoping to get away early today; just goes to show.' She was a tall, slender woman, with short-cropped hair, just a trace of lipstick as her only make-up. 'Just goes to show: no rest for the wicked. What have you got for me, Chief Inspector?'

'Young, very young, male . . . Life is pronounced extinct. The police surgeon has identified two bullet holes.'

'What appear to be bullet holes,' Dr D'Acre corrected Hennessey. 'Don't stick your neck out; it's dangerous.'

'What appear to be bullet holes.' Hennessey escorted the pathologist to the tent, as for the second time the constable stepped aside. Dr D'Acre stepped into the tent; Hennessey remained outside.

Fifteen minutes later she emerged, angrily brushing flies away. 'Pity, they are so useful,' she said.

'The flies?'

'Yes. They can smell rotting flesh from two miles distant. Start laying eggs – very useful in establishing time of death; and we wouldn't be alive if it were not for them.'

'We wouldn't?'

'No. They and other insects are the bottom of the food chain. Everything above depends on them; otherwise it would be easy to get irritated by them. There's no denying their use . . . so you find yourself being indebted to them. Can be difficult at times to feel indebted to something buzzing up and down your windowpane, but there you are. Well, I have taken a rectal temperature reading and a ground temperature reading . . . All done here. So, if you have taken all your photographs, you may remove the body to York District. I'll have to conduct the post-mortem tomorrow. Eric will be away home by now and I need his assistance. Will you be observing for the police, Chief Inspector?'

'Probably . . . no, certainly,' Hennessey replied.

'Good. Shall we say nine thirty?'

'I'll be there.'

'Again, good.' Dr D'Acre walked away; Hennessey admired a well-toned and muscular body, still lithe, slender and feminine.

'Sergeant!' Hennessey turned to the uniformed sergeant. 'Body bag and stretcher, please, then we can vacate this scene. I assume the sweep found nothing?'

'Nothing at all, sir.'

George Hennessey drove home. He felt irritated, as he had said to Yellich. The Percival–Saffer inquiry was building up a very handsome momentum and now another murder, a very recent murder, had occurred, and that would need to have all resources devoted to it. Home seemed to be inviting for George Hennessey that particular late afternoon in midsummer. He drove cautiously out of York on the A19 to Easingwold and to a four-bedroom detached house on the Thirsk Road at the north end of the town.

He turned into the driveway, and the sound of the car tyres crunching the gravel set a dog barking within the house. Hennessey let himself in and was warmly and excitedly greeted by a tail-wagging brown mongrel. He made himself a mug of tea and he and Oscar went outside to the back of his house, where he sat in a wooden chair on the patio watching Oscar crisscross the lawn, having picked up a scent. A dog flap had been built into the back door, allowing Oscar unlimited access to the garden in Hennessey's absence, but it was Hennessey's observation that the animal preferred to be indoors during that absence, and enjoyed the garden only in his presence. He pondered the garden, the lawn, the hedgerow growing across the lawn with a gate set midway, the potting sheds beyond the hedge, two side by side, and the orchard, also beyond the hedge, and beyond the orchard, the area of waste – or the 'going forth', as Jennifer had called it – and the pond therein. He finished his tea, poured tap water into a bucket and took it down the garden, followed by a curious Oscar. Seeing, as anticipated, that the pond water had largely evaporated, he poured the water into the shallow, muddy soup. Four more bucketfuls of water were required to replenish the pond. He sat again in the wooden chair whilst Oscar found shade by the hedge and sat looking at him, occasionally wagging his tail.

'Busy day today.' He savoured the warmth of the sun's rays. 'A couple of useful visits in respect of the Percival–Saffer case, which I told you about yesterday; then a new case right at the close of play, so far as a police officer has a close of play. I remember during training how we were told that a policeman was never off duty, so I suppose the only close of play I will have is my retirement. That is not so far off, and at least it looks like I am going to make it, unlike the youth who was found in the wood earlier today . . . Still in his early twenties, everything ahead of him, everything to live for. Shot twice . . . very neatly . . . dare say Eddie Challis would approve. Remember he's . . .' Hennessey's voice faded; he fell silent; then he said, 'It's gangland. It's a gangland job. That's why I enjoy talking to you: I realize things – and this is just one such occasion. I bet we'll know that boy . . . petty crime, I should think. He didn't look old enough or hard enough for anything serious. SOCO took his prints; there'll be a result in my pigeonhole.' He paused. 'In other respects, my social life – well, that seems to be calm and settled. I haven't introduced my lady friend to Charles yet . . . He has asked to meet her. I am very fond of her and I think my feelings are reciprocated, but you must know that you will never be replaced in my life.' Again he felt a warmth settling around him that could not be explained by the sun's rays alone.

Later he cooked himself a simple but wholesome meal of pork chops and vegetables and, while digesting the meal, read further from a book about the Battle of the Atlantic, which he had recently acquired as part of his collection of military history. Later still he fed Oscar and then took him for their customary evening walk, half an hour out, fifteen to twenty minutes exploring a field and small woodland, and half an hour back. Then, later still, Hennessey strolled into Easingwold, enjoying the summer's evening of darting bats and, higher in the sky, circling swallows, for a pint of brown and mild at the Dove Inn – just one, before last orders were called.

It was Tuesday, the third of June, 22.30 hours.

Four

Wednesday, 4 June, 09.30 hours – 19.53 hours
in which a young man's life and death are explored and the gracious reader learns more of George Hennessey's demons.

'Tragedy.' Louise D'Acre looked at the corpse as it lay on the stainless-steel surface, one of the four dissecting tables in the room, a starched white towel having been draped over the genitalia. 'I mean every corpse that comes into this room is a tragedy in that the death has been sudden and unexpected, but some are just more tragic than others. The younger they are, the more tragic, and here a young man . . . with everything before him . . . fit, healthy, good-looking too. The girls would have gone for him all right and he is here. Someone will be weeping, if not now, then very soon. Well-manicured fingernails, neat, clean hair, clean body . . . no young down-and-out drug-abuser here. He lived cleanly and apparently soberly; firm, flat stomach . . . not a great drinker of beer . . . muscular legs . . . the legs of an athlete. Do we have an ID, Chief Inspector?'

'Not yet, ma'am.' Hennessey, standing against the wall of the pathology laboratory, wearing green-paper cover-alls from head to toe, leaned forward slightly as he replied. 'His fingerprints have been taken, but no result as yet.'

'Well ' – Dr D'Acre adjusted the anglepoise microphone that was attached to a ceiling mount so that it was just above and in front of her – 'this is an unnamed case, Sophie,' she said, clearly speaking on to a tape. 'Please give it the next serial number and the date, the fourth of June. Thank you. So, Eric . . .'

'Yes, ma'am.' Eric Filey stepped forward. He was a portly young man; he had an enthusiasm and a strong sense of humour that Hennessey had found to be most unusual among mortuary assistants. All such men in his experience had been gloomy, humourless – 'dour', as the Scots would say. But not Eric Filey, who radiated warmth in the pathology laboratory, like a ray of sunshine, thought George Hennessey.

'We need to shave him.'

'Shave, ma'am?'

'Yes, his head, just here . . . do you see?' Dr D'Acre pointed to the side of the man's head, just above the left ear.

Eric Filey walked round the top of the table and looked where Dr D'Acre pointed. 'Ah . . . yes, ma'am.'

'Shave the scalp hair there, exposing the gunshot wounds, then photograph the area, in colour and black-and-white . . . They will be the cause of death, but we had better have the wounds photographed before we remove the scalp and the top of the skull.'

'Very good, ma'am.' Eric Filey turned, went to an anteroom and returned with a razor, shaving cream and a bowl of hot water.

'He's had his appendix removed.' Dr D'Acre placed her hand on the man's lower stomach as Eric Filey applied shaving cream and began to shave the head as assiduously as a hairdresser attending a valuable and well-tipping customer.

'That might be of use,' Hennessey replied. 'It may help

in identifying him, but if he is as clean-living as you say . . .'

'Yes . . . he's well integrated; someone will already be missing him. You will not, I think, have difficulty establishing his identity.' She turned away as Eric Filey reached for two thirty-five-millimetre cameras that stood on the bench that ran the length of the laboratory.

'Seems not, ma'am.' Hennessey too closed his eyes as Eric Filey lifted one of the cameras, and he kept them shut until the cameras had stopped clicking.

'All done, ma'am.' Eric Filey turned from the corpse and returned the cameras to the bench.

'Very well.' Dr D'Acre turned to the body that lay on the dissecting table. 'Two bullets, two entry wounds . . . no suicide you, young man . . . you didn't volunteer for this . . . you were a pressed man.' She paused. 'The body is that of a young northern-European male in his early twenties. The body is well nourished and well maintained; the muscle tone is good and the body is clean. There is indication of earlier removal of his appendix. The scar has fully healed so that operation was undertaken many months, probably years ago . . . though he is on the young side for such an operation. The scar is not remarkable. There is extensive bruising about the body. The only other evidence of trauma are two bullet entry wounds to the left side of his head above the ear. They will probably prove to be the cause of death . . . but we will see. Rigor is established and this, together with the rectal temperature obtained at seventeen-o-three hours yesterday of five degrees Celsius when the air temperature at ground level was thirteen degrees Celsius would indicate that he was killed four to six hours earlier.' She turned to Hennessey. 'But that is a very, very wide time window, given that he is recently deceased.'

'We have had this conversation before, ma'am.' Hennessey smiled.

'We have indeed. Frankly you can't get better than the mark-one eyeball – the time between when he was last seen and the time his body was discovered is as close as medical science can get . . . so many variables. Corpses actually warm up in the tropics; it's only in higher latitudes that they cool down once the heart stops. That mark-one eyeball observation applies only to very recent deaths, of course: a decayed corpse is a different matter . . . but in this case, our friend here was probably alive twenty-four hours ago and so the police investigation will be able to determine the time of death as accurately – no, more accurately than I could.' She paused. 'Circular saw – no . . . no . . . scalpel, please, Mr Filey; the bullets in his brain are not going anywhere. We'll stay with the issue of the time of death. This won't be too bad . . . not with a small stomach like he has; but you may want to take a deep breath, gentlemen.' Dr D'Acre punctured the stomach with the scalpel and the gas contained therein escaped with a loud hiss. Dr D'Acre stepped backwards as far as the adjacent dissecting table. 'Well, smelled worse, as I said. Are the fans on, Eric?'

'Full on, ma'am.'

'Good . . . we'll give the gases a minute or two.' She waved her arm in the air. 'Had to do a PM on a lady who had been in the river for three days once . . . her stomach was cut here – do you remember, Eric?'

'Yes, ma'am . . . we were very grateful.'

'Yes' – she turned to Hennessey – 'I cleared the lab of Mr Filey and the police who were observing, then just turned away and stabbed . . . then ran out of the room myself; but it was still fully two days before I got the smell out of my nostrils.' She turned back to the corpse. 'Interesting . . .'

'Oh?' Hennessey responded.

'Yes . . . he was hungry when he died, very hungry . . .

71

There is not a trace of food in his stomach and a well-nourished man such as he would have noticed – I mean, felt that absence of food. For a stomach to be as empty as this you are talking forty-eight hours without food, and he is not the type to diet . . . This man liked his food – just look at the muscle tone.'

'What are you suggesting, Doctor?'

'That he was deprived of food for about two days before he was shot. This man was starved. It wouldn't surprise me if you found that he had been held against his will for that amount of time before he was murdered.'

'Interesting.'

'Yes, clean-shaven . . . only post-mortem facial growth . . . and clean . . . That doesn't fit with unlawful imprisonment, but that really is your department. So . . . the bullet wounds' – Dr D'Acre glanced at Eric Filey – 'I think we'll have the circular saw now, please, Eric.'

Eric Filey handed Dr D'Acre a small but powerful hand-held circular saw with which she sliced round the skull, just above the ears. She laid the saw down, thankfully for Hennessey – who felt he would never grow accustomed to the high-pitched whine and the sound of the serrated blade eating into bone – and lifted the top of the skull away, revealing the brain. 'We took X-rays before you arrived, Chief Inspector.' She spoke calmly whilst examining the brain. 'So we know there are two bullets – two holes and two bullets – as we would expect. Saw a case once, one hole and two bullets, in the case of a suicide.' She turned and smiled at him, just briefly. 'Care to hazard a guess as to how that happened?'

'Suicide? So he didn't try twice?'

'No. Healthy brain tissue, as we would expect from one of his tender years . . . You really are too new to be here, young man, whoever you are. No . . . what happened was that the first bullet was a dud.'

'Ah.'

'Went halfway down the gun's barrel then stopped, just lodged there. He clearly was a determined suicide, because despite that reprieve, which might have made me think . . .'

'Me too.'

'Despite that, he pulled the trigger a second time. The second bullet worked as it was intended to work and pushed the first bullet out of the barrel into the man's brain and followed it there . . . So two bullets, one hole, in a case of suicide. Now, we know where the bullets are . . .' She took a metal probe and pushed it into the brain tissue. 'Don't want to do any more damage than necessary . . . The bullets have already done much. Ah . . . got one.' She extracted the probe and took a pair of long tweezers from the instrument trolley and inserted them into the cavity made by the probe. 'Contact . . . hard lock.' She extracted the tweezers, in the jaws of which was gripped one of the bullets. 'Tray, please.'

Eric Filey held a metal tray for Dr D'Acre and she deposited the bullet in it.

'Small . . . harmless looking' – she pondered the bullet – 'hardly larger than the tip of a ballpoint pen, yet so deadly. One would do the trick in the right place . . . two is making sure.' She probed for the second bullet and, finding it, retrieved it with the tweezers and placed it on the tray. 'We'll send them direct to the laboratory at Wetherby . . . but the murder weapon is a point two-two.'

'Thank you.' Hennessey smiled and nodded from his place against the wall.

'That, I think, concludes it . . . In fact that does conclude it. He sustained a prolonged level of violence and was then shot. No other injuries. The brain is very bloody, which shows that the bullets were peri-mortem . . . no or little bleeding in the brain would indicate that the bullet wounds were post-mortem but they are peri . . . very clean . . . very, very clean . . . Yet no food had been consumed for about forty-eight hours prior to death. That, given the well-nourished and very hygienic nature of the body is . . . is . . . strange. There is a story there. People who have been deprived of food for that amount of time, presumably held against their will, are normally quite grubby and with facial-hair growth in the case of males; but this young man was as clean as clean could be. He had a gaoler who had a thing about personal hygiene, so it would seem. I'll trawl for poisons as a matter of course, but my findings will be that death was caused by gunshots to the head and that the time of death may have been yesterday forenoon . . . about . . . and it's a huge "about" . . . nine a.m.'

'Plenty of light,' Hennessey mused aloud.

'Yes.' Dr D'Acre glanced at him. 'That is strange too . . . Sun is well up at nine at this time of year and the place he was found might be woodland, but it is not by any means remote.'

'It isn't, is it?' Hennessey said. 'Just the sort of place a late-middle-aged lady would take her dog for a walk – that sort of convenient open space . . . conveniently close, I mean.'

'Is that how the body was found?'

'Yes – lady walking her dog. It was partially hidden from view, which might explain why it went undetected for as long as it did, but apparently the dog pointed, or so she told the attending officer.'

'I see . . . so, another puzzle.'

Hennessey walked out of the cool of York District Hospital into the glare and the heat of the late-morning sun, which was already creating heat hazes in the car park. He stood, adjusting to the heat, as he watched a hospital porter shimmer though one such haze. Grateful for his panama, he began to stroll away from the hospital and joined the pavement of Wigginton Road and followed it until it became Clarence Street, then narrow Gilleygate. He hugged the shady side of the graceful curve of St Leonard's Place and turned right into Museum Street, where the traffic was inching forwards, bumper to bumper as was always the case in York during the summer, as the city's population mushroomed with the influx of tourists. Again, he hoped that there would not be a fire in the centre of the city. Fires were unwelcome at any time, but Hennessey felt for the nervousness of the Fire Service chiefs; they just could not get an appliance along this street with this volume of traffic, complicated by horse-drawn carriages and road trains taking folk to the Railway Museum. He chose to walk the walls to Micklegate Bar and to the police station. He entered the front doors and smiled as he overheard a constable attempting to give directions to a group of Japanese tourists. He was struggling, but clearly getting there, and so Hennessey left him to it. He opened the 'Staff Only' door and signed in. He checked his pigeonhole and found nothing of importance – just a few circulars, which he read and then consigned to the waste bin. He found Ventnor and Yellich chatting in Yellich's office.

'Busy?' he asked warmly.

'Just about to go for lunch, sir,' Ventnor explained. 'Been doing paperwork all morning.'

'And me . . .' Yellich patted a pile of files on his desk. 'Just waiting to see where we are going with the recent murder. As you said, it tends to stick a spoke in the wheel of the Saffer–Percival inquiry. Didn't want to do any damage, so we both used the morning well for administration.'

'Good, good. We don't know the deceased young man, because the collator would have come back with a result by now if we did know him, so we'll have to wait until he's reported missing. Right, grab some feed, then go back to the Saffer–Percival inquiry.'

'Yes, boss.'

'Go and interview Mule Mulligan. You've read my recording?'

'The driver of the car when Challis drove out to shoot Ralph Brodney? He's under the witness protection scheme.'

'Yes, Challis said he was a twenty-four/seven gofer for Margaret and Duncan Percival. He's had long enough now to do some serious thinking. I've tracked down his whereabouts. Go and see him; he might remember some other details . . . he talked willingly enough back then.'

'Very good, sir.' Ventnor stood. 'We were just waiting for the word.'

'Good.'

'Then go and visit Mrs Brodney; see what she can tell us about Margaret Percival. I'll hold the fort.'

Thompson Ventnor glanced at the lush green and yellow fields, the occasional stand of trees, the occasional farmhouse, and then turned to Yellich. 'What do you know about the Chief?'

'Not very much, really.' Yellich kept his eyes on the road, the A1 – two lanes in either direction separated by a barrier of greater or lesser width, depending on the section of the road. At that moment the barrier was generous: a shrub-covered ditch, which would stop any vehicle crossing from one carriageway to the other, and this made Yellich feel safe. The A1 was one of Britain's most dangerous roads and Yellich, knowing that, approached it with respect. 'We've worked together a few years now and I still don't know much about him. He's a very private man.'

'Not from Yorkshire, by his accent?'

'No . . . he's a Londoner – Greenwich, I think . . . Yes. Is that where the *Cutty Sark* is – the clipper ship?'

'Yes, that's Greenwich – east London, on the bank of the river . . . south of the river. I used to have a friend who lived in Greenwich. Still have her as a friend, but she's moved to Oxford now; better place to bring up her daughter.'

'I see.'

'Where does he live?'

'Easingwold.'

'Not bad.'

'Yes, it's a pleasant little town. Don't know it well but I have liked what I have seen.'

'Bachelor?'

'Who – the Chief?'

'Yes.'

'Long-term widower. He has that careworn look of a bachelor . . . No one to forcibly remove his sports jacket after thirty years' faithful service, to cut it up into duster-size pieces.'

'Yes, that's what I meant. He doesn't seem to have that woman's touch about him.'

'His wife died young . . . I mean very young – in her early twenties.'

'I'm sorry to hear that; that is a tragedy.'

'Yes . . . I don't think he ever will recover. I think it was a blissful union . . . I have that impression.'

'Accident?'

'No . . . no . . . Natural causes.'

'At that age?'

'Yes . . . He did tell me once . . . Sudden-death syndrome.'

'Ah, I have heard of that.'

'Tends to strike healthy people in young adulthood. She was walking down the main street in Easingwold, on a day like today – midsummer – and just collapsed. Folk thought she'd fainted, but she was lifeless and was found dead on arrival at hospital . . . They took her to York District. Left him with a six-month-old son . . . That couldn't have been easy for him.'

'I'll say.'

'Anybody in his life at all?'

'I hardly think so' – Yellich smiled – 'otherwise that old jacket of his would have been condemned as a health hazard years ago. Or . . . perhaps just his wife, inside his head.'

'In his head?'

'Yes. Did you ever meet Tony Tripp – retired a year or two ago?'

'Yes, I remember Tony: angry man; never made it to detective inspector – retired as a detective sergeant . . . got very drunk at his retirement party and gave Sharkey an earful.' Ventnor put his hand to his forehead. 'That was very embarrassing.'

'Yes, I heard about that – pleased I wasn't there; but anyway, Tony Tripp called on the Chief one evening. Didn't get a response from the front door and so went round the back of the house and found him standing on the patio talking to himself.'

'Really?'

'Yes – but he wasn't talking to himself in that sense, like as if he was soft in the head. He wasn't embarrassed about Tony Tripp witnessing it. He explained that he told his wife about his day. Her ashes were scattered in the back garden, you see.'

'I see.'

'So he tells her about his day – each day, upon his return from Micklegate Bar. Quite touching, I always think.'

The remainder of the journey to Durham passed in comfortable but near total silence.

*　　*　　*

Peat Street revealed itself to be narrow, lined on either side with small but neat two-up, two-down terraced houses that abutted directly on to the pavement. The windows of the houses were covered on the inside by net curtains considered infra dig by the professional middle classes of the UK, so Yellich had observed, but which, he also observed, seemed to be a necessity of life for the folk who lived in Peat Street and the likes of Peat Street. The house-holder could see out, but the passer-by couldn't see in, at least during the hours of daylight. Yellich halted the car outside number twenty-three and then, noticing that Peat Street was a cul-de-sac terminating in a massive stone wall, turned the car around so that it faced the open end of the street. Early training had stayed with him: always park your car so that you can make a quick getaway in the event of an emergency and never leave anything in the back of your car that can be used as a weapon against you.

'Quiet,' he said.

'Sorry?' Ventnor released his safety belt.

'The street – it's quiet.'

Ventnor pondered Peat Street. 'It is, isn't it?' A few small cars were parked against the kerb; the sun glinted off their polished bodywork.

'No children playing, yet it is the middle of the summer half-term. A week of no school and there's not a little one in sight. Probably a street of old grey ones. You get that sometimes: the whole street is of the same generation.'

'Probably.' Ventnor wound the window down just an inch so as to allow the car to breathe before he and Yellich left the vehicle and tapped on the yellow-painted door of number twenty-three.

'Gaudy,' Yellich observed as the sound of his knock echoed within the house.

'The yellow?' Ventnor glanced about him. 'It is a bit – the only one of that colour in the street and this fella is trying to keep his head down . . . trying to hide.'

The door was opened cautiously. A tall man dressed in a vest, summer trousers and sandals peered at the officers. He blinked. 'Yes? I was at the back in the yard getting some sun. Who are you?'

'Police.' Yellich flashed his ID. 'DS Yellich and DC Ventnor. We are looking for a Mr Bayfield.'

'That's me. What is it?'

'If we can come in?'

The officers found the interior of the house cool, cosy and pleasantly furnished. The door opened directly into the living room, there being no entrance hall or porch. Beyond the living room was a dining room, beyond that a small kitchen, and beyond that, the back yard with a privy. A staircase separated the living room and the dining room and must have led up to two bedrooms. Both officers were familiar with the type of houses that constituted Peat Street.

'Take a seat.' Bayfield shut the front door. 'It's like the countryside is this street. You don't see anybody, but there's always at least two folk watching you. Do you know the country?'

'Not really.' Yellich sat in an armchair. 'I'm a city kid, really.'

'Me too.' Ventnor sat on a couch.

'It's a quiet street – no young families.'

'We noticed.'

'Just old biddies up to their necks in each others' business.'

Bayfield sat in the vacant armchair beside a small television set, under which were old copies of *Reader's Digest* and Book Club novels. 'So, how can I help you?'

'We really want to talk to Mule Milligan.'

The man paled; his jaw slackened. 'You're not from the Durham police?'

'No. We drove up from York.'

'Are you certain you were not followed?'

'Certain.' Yellich spoke calmly. 'Relax, I drove . . . we were not followed.'

'How do you know? Anyone could follow you on the A1.'

'Yes, but no one followed us off the Durham exit and no one followed us through the town.'

'I'm a dead man if they find me. Eddie Challis has tentacles; he can reach a long way outside Full Sutton. He's after killing me when he gets out. That's what keeps him going: the thought of what he's going to do to me when he gets out.'

'We were surprised you were not further away.'

'There's no point in going any further.' Mulligan shrugged. 'I wouldn't be any safer. I thought about moving south – I mean well south, south of London, like Dover or Folkstone, because I've always wanted to learn to speak French, just enough to get by on, and I thought I would learn it if I could nip across the Channel a few times a month and spend the day in Calais . . . so the language would be real. But I'm not happy in the south; life's too soft down there . . . makes me feel like I'm cheating when I'm down there.'

Yellich nodded. 'Many northerners feel that way.'

'So I came here . . . so long as I am not in York. I'm a dead man if I'm seen in York – dead man anywhere if I am recognized. I won't set foot in York again.'

'Have you changed your appearance?'

'I have.' Mulligan grinned. 'When I was Mule Mulligan I wore my hair in a ponytail, I had rings in my ears – I mean in a masculine way . . . I had a beer belly . . .'

Yellich pondered Mulligan – short, very short hair . . .

no earrings . . . a trim figure.

'I also wear these.' Mulligan extended a sinewy arm to the top of the television set and picked up a pair of heavy, dark-framed spectacles. 'The plastic is plain – just plastic, not lenses – but I wear them when I go out. My eyesight is good; Mule Mulligan never wore glasses. If I get dolled up – a three-piece suit like a bank manager, carry a brief-case – I reckon I could walk past Eddie Challis and he wouldn't recognize me. It's not a risk I am going to take, though.'

'Are you employed?'

Mulligan shook his head. 'Long term doley, that's me.'

'Well, you seem to be surviving. The reason we have called is that we want information about Mrs Margaret Percival. We understand that you were employed by them?'

'I was – general dogsbody. Shouldn't really have been on that job – the shooting of Brodney: the wheelman went down with a bug . . . really ill. I couldn't really handle a getaway car – well out of my depth; but Percival was insis-tent that Brodney had to be shot that night, so I was told to do the driving. I was well out of my depth. Challis, there in the passenger seat stroking his gun with the sort of love that other folks would stroke a cat or a puppy. Then we did the business, or he did the business, and we drove, and the police were on us with the helicopter . . . That light . . . so bright. Challis said to stop the car, he would pull them off; he said they would always follow the guy on foot, not the car. So, like a fool, I did so. Challis legged it. I drove off and the helicopter stayed with me. Challis knew what he was doing; that's why I turned Queen's evidence against him and Percival. Percival had no right to make me the wheelman. I wasn't up to it and Challis sacrificed me to make his own escape. Percival was behind it, but he denied it and Challis backed him up – he said Percival had nothing to do with it – and the jury . . . well, you know the rest. Helped that the car was Challis's motor, in his name. Percival walked, Challis got life, and I got twenty-three Peat Street and a pair of spectacles with imitation lenses.'

'What we want to know is: how much did Mrs Percival know about her husband's business affairs?'

Mulligan shrugged. 'Couldn't tell you. She knew he was a crook, that's for certain, but how much of the ins and outs, I really don't know. I was the driver–handyman of the house: if it falls off, put it back; otherwise leave well alone. Go and pick up the weekly groceries . . . post the mail . . . keep the cars clean – that was my job: never got near the business.'

'Mrs Percival told us she knew nothing of her husband's work, his business. Was that the case?'

'She's not being truthful . . . but exactly how much she did know? I wasn't with them that long – a few months, that's all.'

'Do you know who would want Duncan Percival worked over?'

'He got a good kicking, didn't he? I heard about that – that was before Challis shot Brodney; but Duncan Percival had given the go-ahead before he was put in a coma and had given Challis the money up front.'

'Unusual.'

'No. Percival trusted Challis. He worked for Percival for some time, as a persuader, and he'd chilled a couple of felons for Percival – you know, the type that are never more than missing persons, so there is no murder investigation. But the person that is missing is at the bottom of the North Sea. Percival has a boat moored in a boatyard on the Trent.'

'Really?'

'It's known to the police. It's all in my statement.'

'Remind us.'

'The *Trent Ranger*, a white motor boat. Percival wants somebody rubbed out, Challis and a couple of others pounce on him, take him to the boat during the night, put his feet in a tub of quick-setting concrete, go down the Trent into the Humber, out into the North Sea, wait until dark . . . the guy goes over the side. Return the next day – just done a bit of night fishing, you see. The guy is reported missing, but without a body . . .' Mulligan opened his palms. 'What can you do?'

'Not a lot.'

'So many people would want to give Percival a kicking. A lot in the underworld – in gangland; but I couldn't name a name.'

'Who could name a name?'

Mulligan shrugged. 'Challis, but he's cagey: he won't tell you anything unless there is something in it for himself. He's a real one-way street, a real Yorkshireman: see all, hear all, say nowt; eat all, drink all, pay nowt . . . and if tha ever does owt for nowt, do it for thysen.'

'I see.'

'Anyone else?'

'Only Mrs Margaret Percival. Whiter than white on the outside, but the core is black. So she'll be cagey, like Challis.'

'What was Percival's business?'

'Still is . . . She will have taken over. Extortion mainly . . . protection money . . . maybe he bankrolls jobs; but that's all in my statement. I don't see how I can help you. You seem to me to have come a long way for nothing.'

Driving south Yellich said, 'He was right.'

'About what?' Ventnor glanced at Yellich, then returned his gaze to a derelict farmhouse, just catching the image as they drove past: a lovely redevelopment project, he thought . . . remote, though.

'About it being a wasted journey. Probably the Chief was right to ask us to visit him, but he didn't embellish his statement at all.'

'Didn't, did he? Got us out of York for the afternoon, though' Ventnor smiled. 'And we need an occasional rest on the company's time. Gives you the impression that you are getting something back – something more than just the pay advice on the sixteenth of each month.'

'I'll come out and speak to him.' Hennessey put the phone down gently, collected his notepad and stood up. He walked down the CID corridor and entered the reception area by the enquiry desk. He steeled himself, knowing this was unlikely to be an easy task. He opened the door to the reception area and saw the man sitting on the bench, as if having been invited to take a seat by the constable, and in his features he saw the youth that had yesterday been found in Plantation Wood. The profile was similar, the build – an aged version, perhaps, but the similarity was there. Father: son.

'Mr Hughes?'

'Yes, sir.' The man shot to his feet. He was smartly dressed, as if having 'dressed up' to go to the police station in the same way as he might 'dress up' to go to chapel on Sunday evenings – very smart in a humble, low-income manner.

'I'm Detective Chief Inspector Hennessey. Would you like to come this way, please?' He led Hughes to the interview room at the far side of the reception area, opening the door for him. 'Please,' he said, as Hughes was clearly awaiting the invitation to sit down.

The two men sat down in upright chairs, which faced each other across the metal table. Hennessey allowed

Hughes to glance at his surroundings: the hessian carpet, the dark-orange paint on the lower half of the wall, the pale-yellow above, the filament bulb attached to the ceiling, the thick, opaque glass windowpane. Then he asked how the police could help him.

'It's about Walter.'

'Walter?'

'My son . . . he's missing. It's not like him to go wandering.' Hughes had a rich, mellow Yorkshire accent. 'We tried to report him yesterday but we were told to wait for twenty-four hours.'

'Yes. We take reports of missing children as soon as they are noticed missing, but adults . . . we wait for twenty-four hours, because most turn up within that time.'

'Well, Walter hasn't and it's been more than twenty-four hours.'

'Yes.'

'Yes?' Hughes held eye contact with Hennessey. 'Do you know something, sir?'

'Mr Hughes, I may have some bad news for you . . .'

'Oh . . .' Hughes's head sank. 'This will be the end of Mary; I know what's coming. She hasn't a strong constitution at the best of times. I can soldier on, but Mary . . . We were elderly parents, you see, sir.'

'Yes.'

'We valued Walter more than we would've done if we'd been in our twenties when we had him, but we were in our forties and Mary thought it was too late for her.'

'I see,' Hennessey said; 'but it's only a possibility I may have bad news for you. I have to tell you that a body has been found – the body of a young man who fits the description of your son.'

Hughes groaned. 'It will be him; I've had a terrible sense of foreboding for the last two days. It's a terrible thing to lose a child.'

'Do you have a photograph of your son, Mr Hughes?'

Hughes opened his jacket, took a photograph from the inside pocket and handed it to Hennessey. Hennessey tried not to betray anything by his reaction to the photograph, but he was clearly unsuccessful, because Hughes said, 'So it is him? I saw it in your eyes.'

'It may be. Can I keep this?'

'Yes – we have plenty and we have the negative of that, so yes, do . . . but it is him.'

'It may be, Mr Hughes. Tell me: did Walter have his appendix removed?'

'Yes, when he was nineteen, as an emergency. Why? – is there an appendix operation scar?'

'Yes, there is . . . It is looking like it's Walter. I can only repeat my condolences.'

'Can I see the body?'

'I'm afraid that won't be possible.'

'I thought . . . you know, on television . . .'

'I . . . We had to do a post-mortem I'm afraid.'

'A post-mortem! You mean he was cut up?'

'Yes. The death was suspicious; we had to do a post-mortem before we could determine his identity. I am very sorry.'

'But how will you know who he is?'

'Well' – Hennessey held up the photograph – 'with this full frontal of his face . . . grinning . . . his teeth can be matched up, as can his hair if we find a sample from his home.'

'Oh . . . DNA? I have read of that.'

'Yes, with DNA we can be one hundred per cent sure that the body is or is not that of your son.' Hennessey paused. 'But I would advise you not to build up your hopes . . . I am very sorry.'

'This is a bad day.' Hughes shook his head. 'You'll have to go to his flat – he moved out of our house a while ago.'

'What is the address?'

'Churchway, Osbaldwick . . . number seven, the top flat, seven E, to be precise.'

'Do you have a key?'

'No, he was very private. I said "was", not "is" . . . Mary won't be able to do that – not easily . . . not Mary.' After a period of silence Hughes asked, 'How did he die?'

'He was shot.'

'Shot! Oh . . . that news item? We watched it on television.'

'Yes. I can't say any more, but if it does prove to be your son who was shot, we'll ask you for all your help.'

'Of course . . . of course.'

'How did you know he was missing, if he doesn't live with you?'

'We live on the same estate, round the corner on Tranby Avenue. I call each week on my way to the Legion, for lunch. Wasn't there two days ago – nothing to worry about; but not there yesterday as well . . . and not away on holiday or anything like that. That was when I knew he was missing. Phoned the police for advice and was told to wait twenty-four hours, then report him missing. So here I am . . . This will be the end of Mary.'

'What did your son do for a living?'

'That I don't know, sir – he would never say; but he had money . . . really nice clothes, but kept odd hours – home during the day, out at night . . . I mean, to work. But he never said what he did – wouldn't ever say.'

'Well, we'll take a drive over to his flat.'

'Shall I come, sir?'

'No . . . no . . .' Hennessey stood. 'I'll have a car take you home. I think your wife will need you.'

'Aye' Hughes stood. 'I'll go and be with Mary, but I'll walk if you don't mind.'

'Not at all.'

'The car journey would be too quick; I need time . . . I need to walk.'

'Of course . . . Thank you for coming in.' Hennessey held the door open for him.

Hennessey and the two constables surveyed the flat. It was, they felt, a scene of mayhem, of chaos. It seemed to have been a neatly kept flat that had been the scene of extreme violence: upturned chairs, television on the floor, splintered coffee table.

Hennessey turned to the nearest constable. 'Better get SOCO here; this is a crime scene.'

'Yes, sir.' The constable reached for the radio attached to his collar.

Hennessey explored the flat: a bedroom, a living room, kitchen and bathroom – quite compact and ideal for a young, single person. The kitchen was neatly kept, the bed was made, the clothing in the wardrobe was hanging neatly, shoes in the hallway were arranged in polished pairs. The man had expensive tastes, Hennessey observed: Italian suits, expensive watch beside the bed. He then began to believe he knew what Walter Hughes did in his strange unsocial hours of working. Gangland has its lure for young men: easy money, a bit of excitement; but the downside, well . . . Hennessey pondered the mess that was the living room. The downside was that you were outside the protection of the law; if someone decided that you were to be iced, then you were iced. The question was: who had Walter Hughes been working for? Leaving the constables in the flat guarding the crime scene, he walked across the landing to the adjacent flat and tapped on the door.

'Well, I didn't hear anything.' The man was elderly, smartly but casually dressed. 'But then I wouldn't.' He indicated his ears. 'I'm deaf . . . I can hear a little if it's close enough or loud enough, but only then. I had to read your lips to understand you. Person to ask is Dolly, below.' He pointed to the stairs. 'Flat beneath Hughes's flat. She doesn't miss anything.'

Dolly revealed herself to be a small woman whose eyes reminded Hennessey of those of a bird of prey. He showed his ID. and introduced himself.

'That'll be the fight.'

'The fight?'

'The other night – dreadful racket: furniture being smashed, shouting . . . ruined my television.'

'When . . . exactly?'

'Late . . . eleven o'clock . . . near twelve . . . but not after midnight. I'm always abed by midnight. Used to work shifts on the railway, used to enjoy the night shift, being awake when everybody else was sleeping; there's a calm about the night, about three in the morning . . . but you sleep during the day, and me – I could never get used to going to bed and getting up on the same day, so now I always make sure I'm abed by midnight. But I was up, so it was before midnight – but late.'

'What programme were you watching? Can you remember?'

'Aye . . . it was ruined by them upstairs. It was *The Fugitive.*'

'That'll help us pin the time down. When was this?'

'What's today?'

'Wednesday.'

'Wednesday?' She raised her eyes, looking past Hennessey as if in thought or applying her mind to calculation. 'Then it was Saturday.'

'Saturday!'

'Yes, because I was watching the film on the television.'

'Sorry – you are Mrs . . .?'

'Miss Dolly Warham – never wed. Not bothered about that now; used to be, but not now.'

'You didn't report the disturbance?'

'No' – she shook her head – 'left that for someone else to do and this is Osbaldwick. Friday nights, Saturday nights, you are sure of a row on this estate. What did you call it?'

'A disturbance.'

'Well, that's the posh word for it, but it happens every week on this estate – raised voices, screaming, smashing windows – then it's all calm again in the morning and they're all nice as ninepence to each other. So if that's family life, you can keep it. That's why I am pleased I never wed. Been courted, though . . . but never wed.' She was smartly dressed; her flat, so far as Hennessey could see, was neatly kept. It smelled strongly of air-freshener and furniture polish.

'Did you see anything?'

'No – only heard him shouting, "It wasn't me," and "Please," like he was pleading for his life.'

'And you didn't phone the police!'

'Thought someone else would do it, like I just said; besides, my phone's there' – she turned and pointed to a red telephone on a small table – 'and I was in the other room. I'd have had to get up to make a call.'

'Well, thank you. I am sorry your viewing was disturbed.'

Miss Warham turned on her heels and slammed the door behind her. Her flat was her den, thought Hennessey as he crossed the landing to knock on the adjacent door, and nothing gets in there – even life-or-limb emergencies.

No other person who lived on the staircase that was seven, Churchway, Osbaldwick admitted having heard any disturbance on the late evening of Saturday last. Hennessey crossed over Churchway to knock on the door of those who lived opposite. The whole of the short street would have to be called on – that would be a job for Yellich and Ventnor the following day; but that evening Hennessey contented himself with the address in question and the house opposite.

'Bottle-green Range Rover.' The man held his door open wide; he was dressed in a blue T-shirt and tracksuit bottoms – early middle-aged, trim figure, broad chest. He impressed Hennessey as a man who not only enjoyed good health but enjoyed enjoying it. He had an eager expression, closely cropped silver hair, and lived opposite number seven on the ground floor. He answered enthusiastically when Hennessey asked if he had seen anything unusual on the night and at the time in question.

'Bottle-green Range Rover?'

'Yes, and a black Mercedes.'

'Here?'

'Yes, in Osbaldwick – dole city . . . I'd say that's unusual.'

'So would I.' Hennessey took his notepad from his pocket.

'Where were they parked?'

'They weren't; they were leaving the estate Saturday night. I'd been out for the day with the wheelers – a hundred-and-thirty-mile triangle.'

'A one-hundred-and-thirty-mile triangle? You can cycle one hundred and thirty miles in a day?' Hennessey was impressed.

'Yes, easily. We meet at the Minster at nine a.m., get back late. We have stops on the way. Last Saturday we did the coast road – very popular run with the wheelers this time of year. York to Malton . . . Malton to Scarborough . . . an hour or two in Scarborough for a light lunch – mustn't eat too much when you're cycling: get cramp.'

'I can imagine.'

'Then down the coast road to Filey, on to Bridlington, then down to Hornsea . . . Then back inland to Beverly.

Tea in Beverly and a walk round the town, like we walked round the other towns . . . Then at dusk we set off for the last stage – Beverly to York.'

'You wait until dusk?'

'Yes, we always do; we want to extend the day as much as we can, so the last leg is done after sunset. It makes home feel more welcoming. This is about the time of the solstice – in fact it's the anniversary of D-Day the day after tomorrow.'

'So it is.'

'So we might not have left Beverly until nearly ten p.m. It's two hours from Beverly to York by bike, so I was turning into the estate about midnight when these two monsters came barrelling out of the dark – no lights, just missed me. Done all those miles just to get crunched on my own doorstep . . . just imagine that. I'll say that's unusual. Then my neighbour told me about the battle at the top of number seven. Haven't seen that lad that lives there for a few days. Is he all right?'

'No' – Hennessey shook his head – 'sorry, he isn't. We believe he is dead.'

'Dead!' The man gasped. 'But he's so young.'

'Yes . . . We are still a tad short of a positive identification, but any information . . . Did you get a look at the occupants? Any glance at the registration, even partial?'

'Sorry.'

'Or a distinguishing feature . . . of either car?'

'Again, sorry – all over in a flash . . . no lights, and the street lamps here are not the best.'

'What sort of Mercedes was it?'

'The big one – the biggest there is . . . a real sledge.'

'Yes, I know the one you mean. Black, did you say?'

'Yes' – the man nodded – 'definitely.'

'Thank you.' Hennessey pocketed his notebook. 'Thanks, this is very useful.'

'Glad to be of help. Not many folk round here will have noticed anything. I can imagine how that must be, but I'd like to think folk would see something if I was in lumber . . . so I do what I can.'

It was Wednesday, the fourth of June, 19.53 hours.

Five

Thursday, 5 June, 09.30 hours – 22.17 hours
in which Shored Up is met again, a career criminal is called on and Yellich, Ventnor and Hennessey – these three – are at home to the appreciated reader.

'We took samples of his hair from a comb we found.' Hennessey sat forward at his desk. Yellich and Ventnor sat in the upright chairs facing him. Each man cradled a mug of tea. 'They were sent post-haste to Wetherby – we ought to get a response later today. Fresh murder: they'll give it priority; but a photograph provided by his father – that was proof . . . It was a photograph of the same boy I saw in Plantation Wood, so the response from Wetherby will be a positive match. We are now investigating the murder of Walter Hughes, aged twenty-two years. There was a fight, a disturbance, in his flat on Saturday late p.m. – that is the thirty-first of May. A black Mercedes S Class and a green Range Rover, the new type, were seen leaving the estate at speed at about the time of the disturbance. They'll be connected. He was probably in one of the vehicles – nay, certainly he would have been in one, kept against his will until he was murdered by a double gunshot wound to the head – small calibre – a few hours before he was found by a dog-walker on Tuesday afternoon, third of June. He was clean-shaven but hadn't eaten for a day or two before he was killed. So hotel-standard prison, but no food therein.'

'Weird.' Ventnor stole a glimpse out of the window of Hennessey's office: the walls bathed in sunlight, already thronged with tourists in brightly coloured clothing.

'Seems to be a punitive action,' Hennessey added. 'Apparently he was heard saying, "It wasn't me."'

'He was mixed up in something.'

'Seems to have been.' Hennessey smiled. 'You don't get into the gang without proving yourself.' He picked up a sheet of paper.

'We know him?'

'Oh, yes; collator gave me this when I arrived this morning. He was putting it in my pigeonhole as I arrived, so he handed it me instead. Remember a positive ID has still to be made; the DNA match will be positive, but we must wait until we receive confirmation . . . But if it is Walter Hughes, as we know it will be, then yes, he's been a bad lad.' Hennessey paused. 'Assault, GBH . . . so he's keen to prove he's a hard man . . . Possession with intent to supply . . . and he served the complete sentence – three years. He didn't deal with the authorities to reduce his time inside, so he can keep his mouth shut.' Hennessey tapped the paper with his fingernail. 'Classic – classic apprenticeship into gangland: hard man who isn't afraid of a fight, who can keep his mouth shut and demonstrate loyalty to the gang, and all over by the time he's twenty-two. Started at fifteen – car theft . . . He knew what he wanted to be all right – where he wanted to be – at the age of fifteen.'

'A career criminal,' Yellich offered.

'Exactly.' Hennessey nodded. 'A career criminal, a blagger; and that helps us: he is cross- referenced to quite a few names here, all also known to us . . . one or two I recognize. But all will have to be visited. Find out who he has been associating with and if they have a Mercedes or a Range Rover or both. So that's a job for you two – joint visits.'

'Yes, boss.'

'Feel your way as you go . . . Anything and everything about Walter Hughes.'

'Got it, boss.' Ventnor reached forward and took the sheet of paper as Hennessey handed it to him.

'I'm going to visit Mrs Hilda Brodney, keep the Percival investigation alive. Hughes has to take priority, but I don't want to lose sight of the Percival case. We'll rendezvous back here after lunch.'

'How did you find me?' Hilda Brodney seemed to Hennessey to have sought to retire from life. She was pale, thin, dressed haphazardly, with untidy hair.

'The estate agents.'

She nodded apathetically. Hennessey thought that a person with more spirit might have been angry at her address being given out by an estate agent, but it was a further sign, Hennessey felt, that much of the will to live had left the woman.

'They were obliged to,' Hennessey explained. 'It was part of a murder inquiry. I went to your old home . . .'

Mrs Brodney groaned. 'My old home. I so loved that house. Now I live in this.' She indicated her present home. 'I had cupboards larger than the rooms in this . . . shoe box.'

'The present owners didn't know your address; they told me that they forwarded any mail for you to Cooper and Smith's.'

'Yes.'

'They were reluctant to give me your address, but, as I said, I told them it was a murder inquiry – they could be forced to give the information. It wouldn't take me long to get a warrant, so they kindly cooperated. You mustn't be angry with them.'

'I'm not. I'm not angry about much at all these days. Do you want to come in? I don't get visitors; even a policeman is welcome.' She turned and walked back into her house. Hennessey followed her and saw what she meant about having had cupboards in Hallam Grange that were larger than the rooms in her present house. It was very small, so small that Hennessey felt as though he had grown in size. It was clearly, he thought, one of the newbuild houses thrown together by unscrupulous builders, who said, 'We are not interested in building houses; we are interested in selling them' – quite a different concept, houses with a design life of twenty-five years, so that when the owner's mortgage was paid off, the house was valueless. Such builders had show houses on the estate with scaled-down furniture to make them appear larger than they actually were.

She led Hennessey though to the living room and seemed to twist and collapse in one movement into a red armchair, which looked to Hennessey no larger than a seat in a small car. She indicated a settee. Hennessey sat down on it, sensing it struggling to cope with his weight. It too seemed small for the job it was meant to do. Hennessey felt that he was sitting on a ledge that protruded from the wall. He glanced out of the window. Just a few feet separated Mrs Brodney's house wall from her neighbour's. Coming to this from Hallam Grange would have made any soul dispirited, so Hennessey mused, and he could understand her despondency.

'A murder?' she asked. She seemed prematurely greying and wrinkled. 'Another one?'

'Yes; it may be connected to your husband's murder.'

'That was my murder too.' She sank back into the chair. 'It seemed I knew more about my husband once he was dead than I ever did when he was alive. That night was the end of my life. I remember it well, as I would do – as anyone would do. Ralph was not as cautious as he should have been – too cocksure, too sure of himself. Car pulled up outside our house – lovely, lovely old house, but you've seen it?'

'Yes. It is indeed a lovely building.'

'That house – it wasn't just a building like this one; it was alive, it welcomed you when you arrived home, it had a warmth. I sensed it the moment I stepped over the threshold and I begged Ralph to buy it. We paid well over the asking price, and I was so happy there . . . but that night a car drew up outside . . . the bell rang . . . Ralph muttered something about it being one of his employees: he was expecting someone to call. He got up to answer the door and a moment later there was an explosion. I had never heard a gunshot before but I knew what it was. Went out into the hall and there was poor Ralph – lying there, blood coming out of his head. Phoned nine-nine-nine and the police – you people – arrested the driver that night just a few minutes later. He named the gunman in exchange for charges being dropped against him, but you'll know that. A creature called Challis murdered Ralph. I sat through every day of his trial – evil, cold-hearted thing . . . a thing. He's not human . . . those eyes . . . that straight-ahead stare of the psychopath. I saw it all during his trial. It was then that my world fell apart.'

'How?'

'Ralph was a fixer; Mr Ten Per Cent – had this deal going and that deal going, always ducking and diving, always bobbing and weaving. He was always like that, even at school. That's where we met. He had a paper round and the newsagent was a young man who went off each morning in his car to deliver his girlfriend's morning paper, leaving the newspaper boys in charge of the shop. They were clever; their thieving wasn't obvious – just forty cigarettes and two magazines and a couple of chocolate bars each. Ralph kept the chocolate to himself but sold the cigarettes and two magazines at school. That was the beginning of his business empire. It wasn't until after he was dead – hardly cold in the ground – that a couple of men called and said they had come to take possession of Hallam Grange – my house, built in 1805, the year that the Battle of Trafalgar was fought. I ordered them out, called the police, but they had papers – turned out that Ralph had sold the house to a finance company to release the equity. He could continue to live in the house, but upon his death or prior removal to an institution the house became the possession of the finance company. He could do that without telling me because Hallam Grange wasn't in joint names. So I was a widow and homeless, all within a week. Then the nature of his business – that was the next blow . . . the long-running feud with Duncan Percival. I knew Percival was a crook but never knew Ralph was as well. I thought Ralph was a bit of a wide boy, but not a criminal – extortion, robbery, fighting the Percivals for control in York and the Vale. If the tourists knew what goes on in this museum town, they wouldn't come.'

'Same in every city, Mrs Brodney: ponder the criminals in London; ponder the millions who visit the city each year.'

'Aye . . . suppose, but it has changed the way I look at York – didn't know then there was such corruption. So, another murder?'

'Duncan Percival.'

Hilda Brodney's jaw sagged. 'He was in a coma; someone beat him to a pulp five years ago.'

'Not quite comatose: he had some consciousness –

virtually no control of his body – but he died of his injuries. His death was directly attributable to the assault he sustained.'

'I see; the old year-and-a-day rule doesn't apply any longer – I remember reading that.'

'No, so it is murder.'

'Well, I can't say I'm sorry; Percival was behind Ralph's murder, which left me penniless. Ralph had no business that I could sell, just a gang of criminals who found work elsewhere. I sold the contents of Hallam Grange to buy this little shoe box.'

'So, you know nothing of the attack on Duncan Percival?'

'Nothing. Ralph kept me well at arms' length. Like I said, I only knew him after he was murdered, but I can tell you one thing and that is that Ralph didn't like violence – not physical violence. You can be violent in other ways besides hitting people.'

'Yes.'

'I found out that Ralph would intimidate, he would blackmail, he would defraud . . . he would commit arson so long as no one's life was in danger . . . he'd steal . . . but he wouldn't harm anybody, nor would he have them harmed.'

'I see.'

'I told the police that at the time. The attack on Percival was a few days before Ralph's murder, but Ralph wouldn't have ordered it – just not his style: that I know; that I did know about my husband. I'd look closer to home if I were you.'

Meaning?'

'Meaning nothing; if it wasn't Ralph who ordered the attack on Percival, who could it have been?'

'Who indeed?'

*   *   *

101

'You seem frightened,' Yellich probed.

'Very,' added Ventnor.

'Do I?' The youth glanced rapidly from one officer to the other.

'Yes.'

'You do.' Ventnor glanced around him. 'Live here alone, do you?'

The youth nodded but said nothing.

Yellich thought it wasn't much of a bed-sit. Very bare – just the basics: a bed, a worn carpet, a wardrobe, a chest of drawers, an easy chair, a view over the back garden. 'Just room for one anyway, eh, Larry? I mean there's others in the house, all paying rent, but just you in this room?'

'That's what I meant.' Larry Mead sat on the bed, holding his hands, pulling at his knuckles. He was twenty-two years old; Yellich thought he could have passed for fifteen. He was pale, skinny, short of stature. Not the sort of person to survive easily in the slammer.

'You don't fancy the prospect of another stay as a guest of Her Majesty?' Yellich asked.

'A what?'

'Another spell in prison,' Ventnor explained, standing next to Yellich.

Larry Mead shook his head vigorously. 'Not going back.'

'You're not?'

'No . . . I . . . They sold me for an ounce of tobacco. I got sold on, from one lag to another. Not going back.'

'You hope.'

'I'm just not going back – done nothing to go back for.'

'So why are you so nervous?' Yellich asked. 'Why are you shaking like a leaf?'

'Cops make me nervous.'

'Not if you haven't done anything to be sent back down the line for.'

'So why are you here? I've kept out of trouble since I was released, and I got out early because of good behaviour. It's not easy living on benefit, but it's better than being inside.'

'Walter Hughes.' Yellich spoke softly.

'Walter?'

'Walter. Seen anything of him?'

'Not for a while. He's a head case. OK, we ran together . . .'

'We know. Got nicked together, went down together.'

'So you're here about Wally Hughes?'

'Yes, we're here about Wally Hughes.'

Larry Mead's head sank in a gesture of relief, 'I thought . . .'

'You've got guilt written all over you, Larry. You've been up to something.'

'Honest . . .'

'We'll find out. Better hope it's not serious or you'll be a commodity again.'

'A commodity?'

'Something that's bought and sold,' Ventnor explained.

Colour drained further from Mead's already very pale face.

'So tell us about Walter "Wally" Hughes.'

'What do you want to know?'

'Everything.'

'Well . . . Wally – he's a head case.'

'We know. Or rather he was.'

'Was?'

'Yes, was. He's dead.'

'Hope you're right about turning your life around, Larry; you've more to fear in prison. Criminals have their own justice. It's a very dangerous occupation, being a criminal. The glamour of the fast lifestyle and easy money has its price.'

'Like a couple of bullets in the head if you tread on the wrong toes,' Yellich explained.

'Is that . . .?'

'Yes, that is' – Ventnor anticipated him – 'that is what happened to Walter.'

'So we're disinclined to mess about. Tell us what you know about Walter Hughes – who he was mixing with, who'd kill him for messing with them.'

'It could help you,' Ventnor advised.

'It could?'

'Yes, it could. You are up to your neck in something, Larry; you reek of it. There'll come a time, there'll come a reckoning, and a good word from us will be of use to you.'

'You're too small-scale, Larry; you don't have the resources to stay ahead of the long arm. We'll see you in the nick, and then you'll need us.'

'We mean really need us.'

Larry Mead looked up at the ceiling, then to his left at the wardrobe, then at the carpet. 'Yes, perhaps I've just done a daft thing . . . You can help me, yes?'

'It's reciprocal,' Yellich said.

'What does reciprocal mean?'

'Goes backwards and forwards.'

'But equally so,' Ventnor added. 'It goes forwards as much as it goes back. So the more you help us, the more you help yourself. We carry weight, myself and Mr Yellich.'

'Mr Yellich?'

'I'm Mr Ventnor.'

'Of Micklegate Bar?'

'Yes.'

'Yellich and Ventnor?'

'Yes; remember those names: they might be useful to you one day soon.'

'Probably very soon.' Yellich took out his notebook.

'Well, you didn't hear this from me . . .'

'Probably, depends what "this" is.'

'Well, I kind of lost contact with Walter. What he was doing was getting too heavy for me; he was running with some heavy boys. I mean, duck and dive; I can bob and weave, but I was getting out of my depth with Walter, so I stopped seeing him – just stopped calling round, didn't want to know too much.'

'Go on . . .'

'Well, he was seeing Dave Scafe – reckoned Scafe could help him get ahead.'

'Scafe? Where do we find him?'

'In your files. He's got plenty of bird under his belt. Plenty.'

'We'll see what turns up.'

'So, this will help me?'

'Depends what we find out from Dave Scafe.'

'It's just that I left my fingerprints behind on something.'

'Not clever of you.'

'No. Didn't intend to.'

'Nobody ever does.'

'See, I thought you had come for me.'

'Not this time, but when we do come for you, just put up your hand to it – none of this nonsense about keeping out of trouble since you were paroled for good behaviour, not if you've left your dabs all over your last job. What was it? A burglary?'

Larry Mead shrugged. 'Mr Yellich and Mr Ventnor.'

'Of Micklegate Bar.'

Walking away through grim and blackened Holgate, Ventnor said, 'I think he was amused by our names.'

'I don't think he has the savvy to be amused by names.'

Yellich smiled. 'But we are a trifle unusual . . . Ventnor –
as in the Isle of Wight?'

'Yes, but we have no connection with the island at all,
so how we acquired the name is a mystery. Yellich is
unusual.'

'Eastern European, we believe, corrupted upon entry
into Britain, the nearest that a hard-pressed immigration
officer could manage. That's how surnames like Ruby and
Diamond appeared in the culture.'

'Really?'

'So I believe. Immigration officers couldn't manage the
Slavic names and so identified an item of jewellery worn
by the immigrant, and Mr unpronounceable and unspellable
became Mr Ruby or Mr Diamond. So we are stuck with
Yellich and know not the original true surname. Where
does your Christian name come from?'

'Thompson? It's a North of England variation of
Thomas. I am Thompson Ventnor the third. Kids at school
found it funny, so I had to crack a few skulls; but I was
well built enough to survive. If I was as sickly as yon
back there, I would have had a harder time. Yours is
Somerled.'

'It's Gaelic, pronounced "sorely" but spelled "S-o-m-e-
r-l-e-d". No Gaelic connection – my parents took a shine
to it. I reckon we are strangely named, but I wouldn't want
to be a John Smith.'

'Me neither. I've grown into my name – very proud of
it now, especially since I am the third Thompson in our
family: grandfather, a cousin, then me.'

A young woman walked towards them holding her head
and smiling. The two officers fell silent as they and the
woman passed each other.

'You know something . . .' Ventnor spoke when the
woman was out of earshot.

'What?'

'Have you noticed the tendency that people in the UK in the early twenty-first century have of walking down the street talking to themselves whilst holding a little box up against one of their ears?'

Hennessey spent the rest of that morning writing up files, catching up on paperwork – tedious at times but, oh, so necessary, as he knew, having in the past bene-fited from accurate data. At lunch time he put on his jacket and panama hat and strolled out of the red-brick building that was Micklegate Bar Police Station, across the road to Micklegate Bar and, grateful for the shade within the stone tower, climbed the stairs on to the walls and walked to Baile Hill, which was the section of the wall he always found to be least occupied and which finished amid an enchanting stand of trees. To his left were well-kept terraced houses and a view over their rooftops to the Minster, which gleamed in the sun, and to his right, more housing, the less desirable 'without the walls' properties. Leaving the wall at Baile Hill, he crossed the Ouse at Skeldergate Bridge. The river, he saw, was of a pleasant blue hue and was busy with summer tourist traffic, from small, two-seater petrol-driven boats to the two-tiered passenger launches. St George's Field and the South Esplanade were thronged with tourists, all brightly dressed and clearly enjoying well-earned rest and recreation. He walked on. His own rest and recreation would have to be deferred. He walked along Tower Street and crossed the sluggish River Foss and into Lead Mill Lane, through low-rise modern housing, and into Hope Street, across Walmgate, into an area of older terraced housing, and turned right into Speculation Street. He walked into the snug of the Olde Speculation at the end of the street. Shored Up smiled as he entered the room.

'First time lucky,' Hennessey took off his panama. 'Here or the Highwayman.'

'Or the Yorkshire Volunteer, or the Royal Oak – one of the four, but all in the same area, quiet and away from prying eyes . . . and seeing you twice in two days – I am honoured.'

Hennessey inclined his head and walked to the bar, where a sullen-looking barmaid waited for his order. He asked for a Scotch and dry ginger for 'his friend' and tonic water with ice and lemon for himself. He was served in a slow, perfunctory manner and was surprised to note the woman wore an engagement ring. He did not envy the man who was intending to become her lifelong partner and was reminded of a cartoon he had seen, the caption of which was: 'I know she's alive, she blinked!'

He carried the drinks over to where Shored Up sat at a corner table, beside windowpanes of coloured, frosted glass.

'Or the Wig and Quill – been in there a few times recently.'

'I'll remember that.' Hennessey sat down and placed the Scotch in front of Shored Up.

'But mostly it's here or the Highwayman.'

'I'll make this and the Highwayman my first port of call whenever I am looking for you. Your good health.' He raised his glass.

'And yours, Mr Hennessey.' Shored Up drank the Scotch lovingly, savouring it. 'So I take it you had no luck in your recent inquiry?'

'Not a lot.'

'Well, two days isn't much time to give yourself, Mr Hennessey.'

'It's not that: the Percival–Saffer inquiry has had to be put on hold. We will still talk to the people you mentioned. I forget their names. I have them written down, though.'

'Toby Murphy and Terry Wales.'

'Yes . . . I really want to pick your brains about the recent murder.'

'Oh, that young man?'

'Yes.'

'I read it – saw it on the local TV news. Shot in the head.'

'Yes, that's the one. It's gangland.'

'Is it?' Shored Up raised an eyebrow.

'Yes, has all the hallmarks, the execution-style of the murder – double tap, I believe it's called: very close and two to make sure; and we believe the young man to have been embarking on a criminal career.'

'How unwise.'

'Very.'

'All long-term criminals are dead, and dead before their time, or in gaol or, like me, in poverty and bouncing in and out of gaol for petty offences. I do wonder about my old age, Mr Hennessey – no pension for the likes of us . . . but too late to start one now. All I can do is hope for the big one, the major score that will provide for me in my declining years.'

'During which time I'll be watching you like a hawk.'

'An occupational hazard I have to live with. Anyway, the young fella – what was his name?'

'Hughes – Walter Hughes.'

'Yes, he was a name beginning to get known. Wally Hughes . . .'

'Wally?'

'Yep, he had a future, he was determined – bit of a hard case; I mean hard in here' – Shored Up tapped the side of his head – 'and hard in here too' – he tapped his chest. 'He had the makings of a big name.'

'You sound like you admired him and his sort. You surprise me.'

'Not admiration, Mr Hennessey; violence isn't my style. Just letting you know what I heard.'

Hennessey sipped his drink. 'As someone said to me just yesterday, you don't just have to hit someone to be violent, and defrauding wealthy widows out of their life savings is a form of violence.' He replaced his drink on the highly polished circular table. 'But anyway, so whose toes had he trodden on? Do you know?'

'I don't.'

'But you could ask?'

'I wouldn't ever do that; I'd get double-tapped myself if I asked.'

'Fair enough.'

'But I will keep my ear to the ground; rumours tend to come my way once in a while.'

'I imagine they do.'

'And one favour will deserve another in return, won't it, Mr Hennessey? You see, my probation officer is awfully keen – new, you see: just out of university. It's like having to report to my daughter.'

'Well, she does have lawful authority. I'd cooperate, if I were you. How many appointments have you missed?'

'Couple.'

'By which you mean about six.'

Shored Up shrugged. 'And there is that outstanding charge I mentioned.'

'But if you help us, I can put in a word – might stop you being breached for failure to comply.'

'I would appreciate it, Mr Hennessey.'

'In that case, perhaps you'd show your appreciation by coming up with the goods. We think a Range Rover and a large Mercedes were driven by the felons who abducted Walter Hughes. The Range Rover is green, bottle-green; the Mercedes is black. Know anyone who owns makes like that, especially as a pair?'

'Confess I don't.' Shored Up tweaked his military-style moustache and Hennessey could quite understand why this man, who seduced middle-aged women by passing himself off as Colonel Smythe (retired), Devon and Dorset Regiment, should find it so difficult to report weekly to his 'daughter' at the Probation and After-Care Office. So very, very difficult, the more he began to believe his own lies – though that perhaps, he thought, was all the more reason to comply with the order and keep the appointments, thus preventing himself from believing his own fantasies.

'But you'll keep your ear to the ground for us?'

'Certainly. Most certainly.'

Yellich picked up the phone on his desk and asked the collator for everything and anything on one David 'Dave' Scafe. Ventnor leaned against the radiator and unwound a paper clip, trying to make it into a near-perfectly straight piece of wire. Eventually he got frustrated and tossed it into the waste bin.

'That's a waste of taxpayers' money,' Yellich observed humorously, as the straggly length of wire bounced against the side of the metal bucket.

'Drop in the ocean, my son, compared to the other waste that goes on in here and the other nicks.'

'That is sadly true.' His phone rang; he snatched it up and pulled his notepad towards him as he did so. 'DS Yellich . . . collator.' He glanced at Ventnor and gave the thumbs-up sign.

Ventnor continued to lean on the radiator as he watched Yellich scribble details on to his notepad. Eventually Yellich replaced the handset and said, 'Got a naughty boy here . . .'

'Oh yes? Do tell.'

'Known to Manchester police and the Met, which goes

to explain why we haven't heard of him. In a small city like York he would be a very big fish.' Yellich glanced at the notes he made. 'He's done time.'

'Age?'

'Forty-three.'

'OK.'

'Time for . . .?'

'Armed robbery, extortion, assault, but armed robbery is the big one: two separate convictions – collected ten years on both counts.'

'And he's only forty-three!'

'Yes, he didn't hang around – first conviction at seventeen. He would have worked towards an early parole each time the moment he got inside the gates. Probably served less than half of the two ten-year stretches, which accounts for his length of track for one so, well, relatively young. According to this, he has spent half his life inside, but these figures mask the early releases for good behaviour; these figures are just his sentence collection. Recidivist is just not the word; this guy only knows crime as a way of life.'

'Where does he live?'

'In the Vale. Small village. Lower Disley – know it?'

Ventnor shook his head.

'Out by Malton way.'

'Lots of money out there.' Ventnor glanced out of Yellich's window at the car park at the rear of the police station and noted how heat rose in shimmering clouds from the tarmac. 'Lot of green wellies . . . lots of Range Rovers, lots of Mercedes Benzes.'

'That's what I am thinking.'

'Shall we pay him a call?'

'Oh, I think so. Better clear it with the Chief first.'

Hennessey, on his return from his rendezvous with Shored Up at the Olde Speculation, listened to Yellich and Ventnor's account of their morning's work and then said, 'Yes, by all means; go and pay a call on him; test the water; see where you get to. Sounds like a felon we ought to know better, especially if he's going to settle here.'

'Walter – "Wally" to his friends. Yes, I was sorry to hear about him.' David Scafe revealed himself to be tall, slim, muscular – probably, thought Yellich, attractive to women. He wore a red shirt with a black bow tie and dark-coloured trousers, black highly polished shoes. 'He had the makings of a good soldier – no, he was a good soldier.'

'Soldier?' echoed Ventnor.

'Yes.' Scafe nodded. He looked out of the wide window of his bungalow at the garden, at the far end of the lawn, where two young women about nineteen or twenty played tennis on a hard court. 'Bought the bungalow a few months ago, asked my . . . my two companions if they wanted a swimming pool or a tennis court. They asked for a tennis court. They're good girls; they do their duty, so I had one made. Dare say they were right; how much use would you get out of a swimming pool in the Vale? I mean, this is hardly southern California. What is the weather like in the Vale most of the year? Cold, windy, snow, hail . . . hard frost. No, a tennis court was the right choice . . . but Wally was a good soldier. He was going to go far. He'd do a mission and do it well. He'd been captured a few times and he never did a deal with you guys: he could keep his lips shut. Yes, Wally was one of the good ones.' He turned back to face Yellich and Ventnor.

'Did he work for you?'

'I wouldn't say that. I just knew him.'

'How?'

'We met a few times. Never knew who he worked for.'

'Could you be more specific?'

'I could, but I won't.' He smiled. 'I am not going to incriminate myself, Sergeant . . . Sorry, I don't remember your name.'

'Yellich.' Yellich glanced round the room – palatial: his own living room, he fancied, could have fitted into it three or four times over; expensive furniture, plasma TV, two DVD players, original-looking paintings on the wall.

'I've been in prison a few times; it doesn't really agree with me. It's a bit like an overcooked meal – can't do anything with it, so I don't wish to compromise myself.'

'Where were you on Saturday night?' Ventnor spoke suddenly.

'Saturday? Last Saturday?'

'Here' – he pointed to the carpet – 'in this house.'

'Alone?'

'Heavens no' – he gestured towards the tennis court – 'my companions were here also . . . just the three of us.'

'They will vouch for that?'

'Of course. Do you want to speak to them now . . . or later?'

'Later,' Yellich replied.

'Well, they live here; I don't think they are planning to leave – at least not in the foreseeable future. So why quiz me about Walter Hughes?'

'Your name was linked with his.'

'Was it?'

'It was.'

'Who by?'

Ventnor smiled. 'We're not at liberty to say . . . We can be cagey too.'

'Oh, I know.' Scafe grinned and revealed a pair of

gold-capped teeth. 'We play the same game, you and me – different sides of the same coin.'

'So what line of business would you say you were in, Mr Scafe?'

'Me? I'm a venture capitalist. I put up money on high-risk ventures, the sort that banks won't lend on – high risk, but high return.'

'Extortion, you mean?'

'No, I mean venture capitalism.'

'Funding crime, then – is that what you mean? Can't do a job without some outlay: weapons, explosives, perhaps a safe house? You provide the outlay; if the job is successful, you get twice the outlay back. If it fails, you get nothing back,' Ventnor snarled. 'We have come across your like before.'

'I don't think your friend cares for me, Mr Yellich.' Mr Scafe eyed Ventnor coldly. Yellich noted a chill in the man's eye, an absence of soul. Cruel eyes.

'Double garage?' Yellich ignored the remark.

'What?'

'Your house. It has a double garage.'

'How very observant of you, Mr Yellich. Yes, I have a double garage.'

'What cars do you own?'

'A Jaguar and a Volkswagen. Both yellow.'

'A VW? Top of the range, no doubt?'

'No, the smallest: thirteen hundred cc – a Beetle, new type. I don't drive it, of course; it's for my girls, Lucy and Veronica. They use it to bring the provisions in. That's part of the agreement: they undertake a few domestic duties . . . as well as . . . well, just as well.'

'I see,' Yellich growled. 'We'd like to check.'

Scafe fell silent as if in thought. 'I don't think there is anything I don't want you to see . . . and you just want to check the cars?'

'That's all. We don't need to go into the garage, but it's interesting that you don't want us to go in. Something to hide?'

'Of course I have: I am a career criminal. Any slip on my part could be the end of me. It's up to me not to make that careless slip.'

'I know – gaol doesn't agree with you,' Yellich said.

'Like an overcooked meal,' Ventnor echoed. 'That's the strangest description of gaol I have ever heard.'

'Just the way my mind works, officers, just the way my mind works.'

'Do you own a gun, Mr Scafe?'

'No.' The answer was quick. Direct. Strong.

'But you'll have access to one?'

Scafe shrugged. 'Might do.'

'Oh, you will.' Yellich spoke softly. 'Why Yorkshire?'

'What?'

'What's wrong with Lancashire all of a sudden? Why settle this side of the Pennines?'

'Just fancied a change of scenery – simple as that. Do you disbelieve me?'

'Yes, I do,' Yellich said.

'Yes, we do,' Ventnor added. 'Let's look at your cars, then we'll be on our way – leave you to enjoy the company of your companions.'

Driving away, after verifying that the cars in Scafe's garage were indeed a Jaguar and a small Volkswagen, Yellich, at the wheel, said, 'We'll be seeing him again.'

'As sure as night follows day.' Ventnor kept his eyes fixed on the road. 'As sure as night follows day and as sure as eggs are eggs.'

Yellich went home. He was pleased as always to arrive. His home was a modest newbuild house in Huntington and Jeremy ran to greet his father and impacted with him with a blow, which Yellich had to brace himself to receive. In the house Sara flung her arms round her husband's neck and kissed him.

'It's been a good one, one of the better ones,' he said, holding her. 'I can tell.'

'Yes, it's been a good one, one of the better ones. George, next-door George – not George in the village – he let Jeremy help him lay the track of his new train set. Not many men would let a boy like Jeremy play with their toy train.'

'Model.' Yellich kissed her. 'It's a model. Don't ever let a model-railway enthusiast hear you referring to his passion as a "toy train".'

'OK, I'll remember that.' She rested her head against his chest. 'But . . . I got through the day because of those two or three hours. Tomorrow won't be as easy. Can't ask, can't expect George to entertain Jeremy for two or three hours every day, besides which they are going out for the day – off to the coast to get some sea air and fresh-tasting fish and chips. So . . . me and him tomorrow. Can't wait for half-term to end . . .'

'One day at a time – it's all we can do. I'll get changed and take him for a walk.'

Later, dressed in jeans and T-shirt, Yellich took his son for a stroll, down Church Lane to the meadow where boys fished for minnows in the stream as older boys, naked to the waist, played football and seemed to know whose side each player was on despite absence of strip. He and Jeremy walked slowly, identifying plants and birds. After an hour's stroll, Yellich said, 'Shall we go home for supper?' To which Jeremy responded with a smile and a nod of his head. Later still, after Jeremy and his father had washed the dishes, they sat down and, using an old clock, Jeremy demonstrated how he was managing to tell 'hard times' like 'twenty-three minutes to three', and 'two minutes past two'. Even later still, when Jeremy was in bed, Sara and Yellich sat together on the sofa sipping wine and listening to Bach's Toccata and Fugue in D minor. They didn't speak; each other's company was all either needed.

Thompson Ventnor had also gone home.

'Divorced,' he said.

'Same here.' The woman smiled. 'Just once . . .'

'Same here – second best, as they say.'

'Indeed.'

Ventnor had changed into a stylish but lightweight summer suit, exchanged his working shoes for a pair of Italian ones and called a cab to take him to the city. He had gone to a couple of pubs to kill time and then, about eight p.m., walked to the Augustus Wine Bar on Davygate. He had ordered a glass of white and carried it over to where the woman sat alone on a high stool at the bar. She was slender, elegantly dressed, in his view, mid- perhaps late-thirties, with long blonde hair – possibly extensions, he thought, if not a wig – make-up a little on the heavy side for his taste and loud taste in lipstick, like a model from the 1950s, he observed. But she was a woman; she was alone, perched on a stool in a wine bar: she was fair game.

But in the end he went home alone. Again.

In Easingwold, just about the time that Thompson Ventnor was entering the Augustus Wine Bar, George Hennessey stood on the patio with Oscar at his feet and looked out over the garden. 'We still don't know who Walter Hughes was working for; answer that and we're more than halfway home.' He then looked down at his dog and said, 'Come on, pal; it's cool enough for you to walk now.'

Oscar responded with a bark of excitement.

* * *

Mule Mulligan lazily responded to the soft, childlike tap on his door. He unlocked and opened it and instantly tried to shut it again with a yelp of panic, but he was too late and had insufficient strength.

It was Thursday, the fifth of June, 22.17 hours.

Six

Friday, 6 June, 09.10 hours – 21.15 hours
*in which a young man is arrested for his own protection
and the Chief Inspector views used motor cars.*

Hennessey broke the silence. 'It's called a "Chelsea
smile" apparently, probably because it was a term
first coined by London gangsters; but the term has stuck.'

'Bit like a "Clydeside screwdriver".' Yellich kept his
head hung low. 'Give someone a hefty blow, it's called a
Clydeside screwdriver. Heard that expression used a long
way from Scotland.'

'It's a penalty reserved for someone who informs or
who turns Queen's evidence – breaks the underworld code:
if he wants a big mouth, we'll give him one – cut open
his cheeks back from the corners of his mouth, then cut
his tongue out and leave it in his mouth. He would have
been alive when that happened – blood everywhere; and
the tongue bleeds profusely when it's cut open – or cut
out.' Hennessey fell silent again. 'Then he was shot.'

Ventnor bent low, head hung, elbows on his knees. 'We
were not followed. I . . . we . . . are sure that we were not
followed.'

'Well, we can follow someone, keeping a few cars back –
using two or three different cars; why can't they? That's
the nature of police work: you never stop learning.'
Hennessey leaned back in his chair. 'Now we have learned

that the felons have copied our surveillance technique and are using it against us.'

'I suppose it's a bit like the country,' Yellich offered. 'You're in the fields, in the woodlands, don't see a soul, but that doesn't mean nobody is watching you; in fact, that's what he said about the street in which he lived.'

'It's a good parallel.' Hennessey nodded. 'Just because you can't see anyone, it doesn't mean to say you are not being watched. The fields have eyes and the woods have ears – isn't that the saying?'

'I'll carry this to my grave.' Yellich turned to Ventnor.

Ventnor nodded his agreement. 'Guilt just isn't the word . . . but we didn't know. We had no reason to believe we were being followed. How would they know which of us to follow?'

'Followed every plain-clothes officer until they realized that they were going somewhere interesting, then whistled up support using their mobile phones,' Hennessey explained. 'Once they realized you were leaving York and going some distance, they must have realized the possibility that you were visiting Mule Mulligan had become a probability. Challis would have set it up – alerted someone after my visit to him, told someone that we were likely to be visiting Mulligan to question him about the Brodney murder and its link to the Percival gang; so all plain-clothes officers were followed.'

'Who is this gang,' Ventnor appealed, 'to have resources like that?'

Hennessey shook his head. 'Monstrous, whatever it or they are: well organized, plentiful, murderous . . . ruthless. What were your impressions of Scafe?'

'Smooth . . . slippery. He talked but didn't give anything away. Getting hold of his personality was like trying to nail jelly to the wall.' Yellich glanced at Ventnor, then at Hennessey.

'Getting him to open his mouth in any way that was useful for us was like trying to open an oyster with a bus ticket,' Ventnor added. 'Tried to tell us he was a venture capitalist.'

Hennessey smiled at the image of the oyster.

'It's not original,' Ventnor conceded. 'I read it once – caption of a Victorian cartoon in *Punch* magazine. Wife complaining to her husband, who won't speak, that getting anything out of him is like trying to open an oyster with a bus ticket.'

'Still, I appreciate the image. Scafe will speak but not of anything of great import. That will have to be prised out of him and, as I said to my wife yesterday evening, we will not get any further forward until we find out who young Walter Hughes was working for. Would he and Scafe be working for the same person?'

'Possibly, boss.'

'Right . . . and we need to find the owner or owners of a green Range Rover and a black Mercedes . . . and we need to find out where Challis links in, if he links in at all; and above all we need to find out more about Walter Hughes and David Scafe.'

'Yes, boss.' Yellich grunted. 'This is York and the Vale of: green Range Rovers are as common as red buses in London; but black Mercedes – and we know the class: "one of those huge sledges" – they are not so plentiful in number. We ought to check local vehicle-licensing – see if the names of any of the owners seem interesting.'

'Yes. Can you do that, Yellich?'

'Yes, boss. Then I think a revisit to Hughes's friend . . . what was his name?'

'Mead – Larry Mead.'

'Yes, go back and see him. You said he seemed frightened.'

'We did . . . and he did.'

'All right: pound to a penny he knows more than he told you. Go back and tell him we want the rest . . . or pull him in for something.'

'Yes, boss.'

'I'll phone Greater Manchester Police, get some more background on Mr Scafe. So, we know what we are doing?'

'Yes, boss.' Ventnor and Yellich stood and turned towards the doors of Hennessey's office. Yellich turned back to face Hennessey. 'Who found Mule Mulligan?'

'Oh, milkman doing his rounds: Mulligan's house was near the beginning of his round; open door – very unusual, and the bloke could see signs of a struggle, so he knocked. No answer; put his head round the door; saw what he saw. The Durham Police contacted his handler, who informed me as soon as I arrived here this morning.'

'Chelsea smile,' Yellich said.

'Chelsea smile,' Hennessey echoed. 'Very messy.'

'Come on, Larry.'

Larry Mead wrung his hands. 'Scafe – he was working for Scafe. I told you.'

'So who was Scafe working for?'

Mead shrugged. 'Last I heard he was working for Percival.'

'Percival's dead.'

'Yes, but not . . . dead dead . . . not in his coffin. He was dodging the coffin . . . but not in it.'

'You are saying he wasn't so much of a vegetable after all – that he was running his business all along?'

'That's what I heard. I wasn't that close to things. Your best bet is still Scafe. Me – I'm small-time – shoplifting, that sort of number; but Walter Hughes wanted more and Scafe was the stepping stone . . . More than that, I don't know.' He glanced round his flat. 'I mean this is all I am . . . but when I think of Wally Hughes – well, it's not bad. It'll do me. If you know too much, it gets dangerous, and I don't have the bottle for what Wally Hughes was chasing.'

'What was he chasing?'

'Big time . . . glamour . . . fast cars . . . women; the quick way to riches, crookin'. Be bent, you can do it . . . you can also get yourself killed. Scares me. I don't know nothing else . . . nothing.'

Ventnor leaned forward and placed both his hands on the arms of the musty, dusty armchair in which the quivering Mead sat, having somehow managed to contract his body to half its apparent size. 'All right, you're not going to tell us any more, that is plain; but I'm telling you, Larry – are you listening? – I'm telling you that if we find out you've been withholding information, we're coming after you and your dainties won't touch. Understand?'

'This is a murder inquiry, Larry.' Yellich kept his distance and spoke in a warm, friendly tone. 'You could be in real trouble. You could be an accessory to murder; that means life. Are you ready for Durham E Wing?'

'That' – Ventnor pushed his face a few inches from Mead's – 'that is where the really, and I mean really, heavy boys go.'

'Very heavy boys,' echoed Yellich, taking the time to glance out of Mead's window at narrow streets and low-rise buildings under a vast blue sky. 'I mean really heavy.'

Mead looked sick; his pallor paled.

'Or Franklin on the Isle of Wight – that's a heavy number too: you have to swim away from there,' Ventnor snarled. 'These are places you are heading . . . or Strangeways in Manchester.'

'Love the name for that prison.' Yellich smiled.

Ventnor fixed eye contact with Mead. 'It's not so funny when you're in there. Cells are smaller than this room and you share one with three or four other guys; wash once a week . . . and the guys who are a long way from home, guys who haven't seen a skirt for years – and you are not an unattractive boy . . .'

'Quite pretty, in fact,' added Yellich.

'You'll be very popular.'

'Make lots and lots of friends.' Yellich smiled. 'Friends like you couldn't imagine . . . all a lot bigger and heavier than you, Larry . . . You're getting quite close.'

'Just a step away, if you are withholding information. And we'll find out if you are doing that.'

'The truth will out,' Yellich said with a smile.

'Thy sins will seek thee out,' Ventnor snarled. 'Or didn't you go to Sunday school?'

'Yes, I went.'

'So you know about right and wrong?'

Mead nodded.

'This is life, Larry.' Yellich spoke in an admonishing tone. 'No one gets out alive . . . and you're on dangerous ground.'

'I've only done daft things.'

'But you rub shoulders with some heavy boys. So how did Wally Hughes get to know Percival? Wally's small time; Percival's no minnow. How did those two get talking? Who made the introduction?'

Mead's head sagged. 'Siddle,' he whispered.

'Siddle!' Ventnor hissed, his face still inches from Mead's. 'Siddle, was that?'

Mead nodded.

Ventnor stood up. 'See, it wasn't so difficult, was it, Larry?'

'I'm dead if they find out it was me.'

'They won't find out – not from us. We can keep our mouths shut.' Ventnor spoke with a hard edge to his voice. 'So tell us of Siddle.'

'Adrian Siddle . . . he's about thirty-five, thirty-six – something like that.'

'Where do we find him?'

'He's got track for this and that, so you'll have him in your computer.'

'That's not what I asked,' Ventnor snarled.

'Where is he?' Yellich asked, still standing behind and to one side of Ventnor, still speaking softly.

'He works for Percival. Driving. So Wally said.'

'So how did Wally and Siddle meet?'

'Inside. Wally was on remand; Siddle was there for a short stretch. Armley that was – over in Leeds.'

'Yes, we know where Armley is.' Ventnor paused. 'You've done a favour for yourself, youth.'

'I have?'

'Yes' – Yellich nodded – 'you have. Wasn't too painful, was it?'

'I met Siddle. He's a nasty piece of work. If he finds out it was me . . .'

'He won't.'

'Only he has this thing he does to folk who open their mouths . . .'

'Oh?'

'Yeah . . . he opens them further. It's called the "Chelsea Smile".' Mead drew his fingertip from the corner of his mouth back across his cheek to the hinge of his jaw. 'Opens them like that. Sometimes they get to live . . . other times they don't. I've never seen it, but I've heard of it. Wally's never known Siddle kill someone, but he's seen someone sliced – had to take part. He held some guy down while Siddle sliced . . . That guy lived.'

'We never heard about that incident.'

'It was in Hull and the guy was too clever to report it to the police. That way he lived, badly scarred and . . . like, branded as a big mouth . . . nowhere to go.'

'All right.' Ventnor glanced at Yellich, who nodded. 'On your feet; we're taking you in.'

'Why?' Mead was alarmed. 'I helped you.'

'It's safer – for you. Stand up. Protective custody. If we arrest you and charge you with a few minors that you'll tell us about, they won't see our calling on you as part of the Hughes murder inquiry. You'll be safer with us.'

'We're learning about these people,' Yellich explained. 'They have eyes – eyes that we don't see. On your feet.'

'So he's fetched up in Yorkshire?' The voice on the phone was male, with a soft Lancashire accent, an accent that Hennessey had always found more musical in some ways than the Yorkshire accent. 'We did wonder where he'd gone, young David Scafe.'

'So, tell me about him.'

'We can fax his file over to you – a copy of same, that is.'

'I'd appreciate it; but if you could give me the gist? I want to take the measure of the man, if I can, as soon as I can.'

'If you can? Not easy: slippery as an eel.'

'So my officers thought. They used words like "wall", "nail" and "jelly".'

'I'll do what I can. This is DCI Staples, by the way – Donald.'

'I'm George.'

'All right, George; well, Scafe is best described as a lieutenant: happy to follow – happier to follow; never seems to have wanted to be the man in charge.'

'I see.'

'Good at controlling a team, good at making sure any mud, in the form of evidence, doesn't land on him or his boss.'

'All right, I get the picture. What's the full track?'

'He started off relatively minor. When he was young he

went inside for affray and receiving stolen goods – that was after a few fines for this and that. He was clearly determined to get some prison time under his belt – a rite-of-passage number. You know how it is: just can't get anywhere in the underworld without prison time on your CV.'

'Yes, I understand all too well.' Hennessey sighed.

'After that he seems to have disappeared for a little while – not quite off the radar, but moved to the very edge.'

'A distant blip.' Hennessey smiled as the expression reminded him of his National Service days in the Royal Navy.

'A distant but significant blip; he was part of the Post Office gang, big in Manchester until they were broken up. Operation Postmistress. A reasonably successful outcome; we were not displeased.'

'I think I read about it.'

'Big crew headed up by two crims called Royle and Mayall . . . hence the "Post Office Crew".'

'And hence Operation Postmistress.' Hennessey laughed at the humour.

'Yes, one of my DC's came up with that name; we appreciated the humour and it was adopted – a two-year operation. The Post Office Crew were tight, very difficult to get near, carrying out armed robberies in the Greater Manchester area. They went down for a total of over three hundred years. Fifteen convictions, in all.'

'We heard Scafe had two long spells inside.'

'Yes, he was something of an enforcer within the crew, a knifeman. It was difficult to get anyone to finger him, but we managed it in the end.'

'And now he's caught up in something again – over our way this time.'

'I'd look out for an alias or two as well. It's not impossible to build a separate identity. I had the opportunity to do it myself once. I often wonder if I would have got away with it. I was a male nurse when I was in my early twenties, worked in a hospital for profoundly mentally handicapped people.'

'Yes . . .?'

'There was this patient, same Christian name as me and same birth year, and in his file was his birth certificate – not a copy but the actual one. Nobody checked the files – just wrote up the nursing notes at the end of each shift. It would have been the easiest thing in the world to purloin his birth certificate on one quiet night shift when I was alone in the ward; then I could have used it to open building-society accounts, obtain a passport in his name. Poor bloke was about three feet long and spent the day resting on beanbags, so he wouldn't ever need a passport. I could have easily returned the birth certificate once I had one or two building-society and bank accounts up and running, and once I had a passport in his name . . . but . . . I joined the police instead.'

'Probably the more sensible decision.'

'Indeed . . . but it does illustrate how it is possible to forge a separate ID which could put someone beyond the reach of a confiscation order. Wouldn't surprise me if he was Scafe aka one or two other names.'

'Interesting.'

'Yes, he seemed to come from nowhere with only his previous to give him a history. I think his previous was in the South of England. Suddenly he's up here as an enforcer and right-hand man to the boss – or bosses. So now he's left the wetlands of Lancashire for the dry lands of Yorkshire. How did he come to your attention?'

'Pretty much the same way as he came to your attention – in the background of bad news: young boy – well, adult male – has been murdered. Scafe's name comes up, he gets a visit and my two officers come away with the impression they have met a slippery customer with much to hide.'

'That's David Scafe, or whatever his name is.'

'Well, thanks. If you'd send the file over?' Hennessey replaced the handset of his telephone as Yellich and Ventnor tapped on the frame of his office door and entered his office. 'You look pleased with yourselves.'

'We are, though it's not funny for young Larry Mead: he's in the custody suite.' Yellich sat in one of the chairs in front of Hennessey's desk, Ventnor in the other. 'You were right: he did know more than he was letting on – gave us another name, one Adrian Siddle, mid-thirties – we are getting his record now; he is known to us. But the interesting thing is that, once again, we have the impression that Percival was running things until of late.'

'In a permanent vegetative state!' Hennessey shook his head, 'I don't think so.'

'Well' – Yellich upturned his palm – 'either he wasn't so much of a vegetable, or he had a caretaker manager . . . probably the latter.'

'Interesting.' Hennessey nodded.

'Also interesting is that Larry Mead, who knew nothing of Mule Mulligan's murder, showed fear of David Scafe and mentioned Scafe's tendency to slice open the cheeks of people who'd been too free with their information.'

'Really?' Hennessey patted the phone. 'That was my opposite number in Greater Manchester. He tells me Scafe was an enforcer and a knifeman.'

'You mean Scafe's in the frame for the Mule Mulligan murder, boss?'

'Well, it has his hallmark; it's beginning to come together. Where is Larry Mead headed?'

'Out to save his skin. We thought it better to bring him in for his own protection, if we are being watched.'

'Yes . . . good thinking.'

'He's coughing to everything but nothing to do with Percival, Scafe, Mulligan, Hughes. So we're getting confessions to receiving stolen goods, car theft, possession of controlled substances. He's telling us what he knows about Percival and Co., but it occurred to us that any information he does give we can say we obtained from Mule.'

Hennessey smiled and nodded gently. 'Again, that is also very good thinking.'

'Thanks, boss.' Yellich consulted a piece of paper. 'You might be interested . . . to check on locally owned black Mercedes S Class . . .'

'Yes?' Hennessey's ears pricked up.

'We might have a result.'

'Oh?'

'One is registered to Toby Murphy.'

'Toby Murphy?' Hennessey looked at Yellich. 'Toby Murphy . . . a bell is ringing. Where have I heard that name before?'

'It's in your recording, sir.' Yellich smiled.

'It is?'

'Following the visit to your informant . . . Shored Up?'

'Ah, yes . . . it's coming back now. He was the car dealer whose business was torched – believed by Percival.'

'That's the one.'

'Again, a Percival connection.' Hennessey leaned forward and rested his elbows on his desk. 'What is happening here? What are we uncovering? The investigation into the murder of Walter Hughes hasn't eclipsed the Percival inquiry – it just leads back to it.'

'Seems so, sir.' Ventnor also leaned forward. 'It seems that Hughes wasn't separate from the Percival gang; he was part of it.'

'So who has been pulling the strings if Percival was a vegetable for the last five years of his life?'

'I think the answer to that question is the same as the question as to who exactly Walter Hughes was working for. So we need to chat to Toby Murphy. I'll do that. I'd like you two to go and lean on Siddle – same sketch as Scafe. Let him know we are sniffing at his tail, take the measure of him.' Hennessey reached for the Yellow Pages: 'Toby Murphy . . . Toby Murphy . . . car dealers.'

'That's the address, sir.' Yellich handed Hennessey the note he was holding: 'Wigginton Road.'

'Ah . . . thanks. The Commander wants to see me later today. I think I know what it's about, but I still have time to visit Mr Murphy. I do loathe second-hand car dealers – that superficial charm, the essential dishonesty of the job, if you can call it a job. "I wouldn't drive three feet in it but 'e went away 'appy'" – which is what I overheard a used-car dealer say in a pub in London once, as a woman curled into his arms, looking like the cat that got the cream . . . but I dare say it takes all sorts.' He looked at his watch. 'All right, lunch. Feeding time first, then we'll pay the calls.'

Hennessey took luncheon at a restaurant opposite the Minster. He found the atmosphere pleasant, the fayre excellent and the price reasonable. He exited the building by the narrow stone doorway and pulled his panama down over his eyes, shielding them from the glare of the overhead sun, which pierced out of a blue and cloudless sky. He crossed the road into Petergate, which was thronged with tourists and street entertainers and, seeking shade and solitude on his walk back to Micklegate Bar Police Station and with a trace of mischief in his mind, decided to make use of the city's snickelways, the series of alleyways that run between the main thoroughfares and are a street system within a street system.

From Petergate he turned into pedestrianized Stonegate and from there he turned left at the Red Devil pub into Coffee Yard, which was, he thought, perhaps the longest of the snickelways, at over two hundred feet, being a narrow and partially covered passageway going past the ancient Coffee House of one Thomas Gent and the former hospice of Nostel Priory, before reaching Grape Lane. Here he turned right into lower Stonegate and entered the cool and quiet snickelway of Hornpot Lane Nether, into St Sampson Square. Once again he encountered crowds of trippers and shoppers, all being pleasantly entertained by two young women in long skirts and T-shirts playing a violin duet, which Hennessey, with his admittedly untrained ear, thought faultless, and he was happy to drop a pound coin into their hat. He entered Feasegate and thence Pope's Head Alley, at the end of which he turned right into Low Ousegate, crossed the Ouse Bridge and began the climb up to Micklegate, to the summit, then descended towards Micklegate Bar Police Station. He signed in, checked his pigeonhole for messages and, finding none, went to his office, where he retrieved his car keys. He signed out again and drove through heavy traffic to Toby Murphy Motors on Wigginton Road. It would have been far, far easier to walk from the restaurant to Toby Murphy's, but he felt he should be seen to arrive by motor vehicle. He reasoned that to do so would give a more assertive impression.

Toby Murphy Motors was easily located, standing on the edge of Wigginton Road. It stood on an area about half the size of a football pitch and contained what Hennessey estimated to be about fifty motor cars, all quality vehicles – Mercedes, Jaguars, Range Rovers, Porsches, Audis, Volvos . . . Wires criss-crossed the area about fifteen feet off the ground and from these small plastic triangles in many colours hung, which would flap noisily in a breeze but on that day hung limply. At the far corner of the premises were an office and a service area. Hennessey stepped out of his car, having parked it in a parking bay marked 'Customers', and began to walk up and down the lines of gleaming vehicles. He located the black Mercedes S Class; it was the only one of its make on the forecourt, and beyond it, just two cars distant, was a bottle-green Range Rover. He looked closely at the Mercedes, peering into the vehicle but not opening the door. It seemed meticulously clean within, as he expected, but he wasn't perturbed: any trace of Walter Hughes having been in the vehicle would be difficult to see, probably microscopic. He turned away and walked to the Range Rover. It, too, was clean, very clean, both inside and out. He plucked his mobile phone from his jacket pocket and pressed the number for Micklegate Bar Police Station. He asked to be put through to Commander Sharkey. He looked about him as the line to Sharkey's office rang. Wigginton Road: close to the hospital, inner-city housing, small terrace houses, corner shops . . . not at all an unpleasant area. He cared not for mobile phones – intrusive . . . amusing only when one was overhearing one half of an argument; but there was no doubt of their usefulness. He could not see a public telephone kiosk from where he stood, and using the radio in the car would have destroyed the game he hadn't thought of playing until the moment he'd seen the parking bay marked 'Customers'.

'Ah, yes, sir . . . George Hennessey here,' he said, when finally his call was answered.

'Yes, George?' The Commander's attitude was clipped, efficient.

'Need SOCO. I am at Toby Murphy's used-car dealership on Wigginton Road – and a warrant to seize two vehicles.'

'You have the registration numbers?'

'Yes sir . . . a moment . . .' Hennessey stood with his back to the office, discreetly glanced at the registration numbers and recited them.

'Got that,' Sharkey said. 'SOCO will bring the warrant in respect of which investigation?'

'The Walter Hughes murder.'

'Young man who was found with two bullets in his head?'

'Yes, sir.'

'Well done, George – that's rapid progress, if the vehicles are relevant.'

'If . . .' Hennessey repeated and then shut the phone off as he saw out of the corner of his eye a smartly dressed man approaching.

'Afternoon, sir.' The man smiled as he closed with Hennessey. He was clean-shaven, in a lightweight blue summer suit, blue tie. He had clearly let Hennessey walk about the cars before walking out to him, not wanting to scare off a prospective customer by being too oppressive and forceful in his sales technique.

'Afternoon.' Hennessey returned the smile.

'All good, clean motors, sir. Can I interest you in one?'

'Yes,' Hennessey replied, 'yes, you can. I like the look of the Mercedes . . . there.'

'Excellent car . . . low mileage . . . a year's warranty, one lady owner . . .'

And her boy-racer teenage son who had sole use of it, thought Hennessey, but said only, 'Really?'

'Yes, really.'

'You don't have a price on the windscreen.'

'Well, that's a bit vulgar, we think, but we would talk around twenty thousand pounds for this vehicle. You'll be trading that . . . car in?' He looked contemptuously at Hennessey's Ford.

'Yes . . . it's a good car . . . but we have come into a little money – you know how it is . . . an inheritance.'

'Yes . . . well done.'

'Well it has solved a problem here and there. You are Mr Murphy of Toby Murphy Motors?'

'I am. A very Irish surname but English as far back as we can trace.' He smiled and revealed a gold-capped tooth.

'Tell me: was this the used-car business that was the victim of an arson attack some years ago?'

'Yes.' Murphy's manner hardened. 'But we bounced back.'

'We?'

'Well, I did, but I find using the plural gives a better impression – more customer friendly.'

'I see.'

'Well, would you like to take a short spin in her, sir?'

'Yes, I think I would – but not quite yet. Can we perhaps go somewhere and talk terms?'

'By all means.' He turned and extended a hand, indicating the office. 'We have links with a finance company that offers competitive terms.'

'Good . . . Which company is that?'

'Percival and Company.'

'Percival?' Hennessey began to walk towards the office. 'Don't think I have heard of them, but then I usually deal with my bank.'

'Yes.'

Hennessey and Toby Murphy walked towards the office. As they approached it, Murphy reached ahead of Hennessey and opened the door. 'Let me get the human flap for you,' he said.

'Thank you.'

Seated in Murphy's office, surrounded by potted plants and a tasteful calendar showing a Ferrari without a naked model draped over the bonnet, Hennessey said, 'Tell me about the Range Rover.'

'The Range Rover?' Colour drained from Murphy's face. 'Why? Are you interested in that car as well?'

'Yes, I am. I am interested in both vehicles.'

He showed his ID to Murphy. 'Sorry, but I am not here to help you move metal.'

Murphy's jaw sagged.

'You look crestfallen, sir.'

'Well, wouldn't you, if a promising-looking customer turned out to be a lawman?'

'So when did you acquire the vehicles?'

'I'll have to look at the paperwork.'

'Off the top of your head?'

'Couple of weeks.'

'So they were definitely in your possession six nights ago?'

'Yes.'

'Do you know anything of the murder of Walter Hughes?'

Toby Murphy sat back in his chair. He looked at Hennessey. He remained silent.

'This is off the record.' Hennessey spoke calmly. 'I have our Scenes of Crime Officers on their way here as we speak, with a warrant to empower us to take possession of both vehicles. We are interested in them because vehicles matching their descriptions were seen in the vicinity of Walter Hughes's house at the time he was abducted.'

'They are not the only Range Rover and Mercedes S Class in York.'

'Granted – but the Range Rover was reported as being bottle-green, the Mercedes black. What is the chance of another bottle-green Range Rover and another black Mercedes S Class being found in close proximity, just one mile from the point of abduction and just six days later? No, those are the two cars we are looking for . . . and you mentioned Percival Finance. That name – Percival – has cropped up like a bad penny throughout the last few days, if not in connection with one investigation, then in connection with another. It's smelling like a tannery on a hot day. I dare say you had both vehicles valeted when they returned, but what could link Walter Hughes to either vehicle may well be microscopic and would survive even the most thorough cleaning operation.'

'Your friends' – Toby Murphy glanced out of his office window – 'I think they have just arrived.'

Hennessey turned and saw two white vans turn into the premises of Toby Murphy's business. 'So they have.' He stood. 'Do something, Toby; you can either work for yourself or against yourself.' He left the office without a backward glance.

Yellich thought it, but Thompson Ventnor said it: 'We've seen you before.'

'You have?' Siddle wore shorts and flip-flop sandals; his bronzed body was well toned.

'We have.' Ventnor nodded. 'Apsley House; you purred up in a BMW soft-top . . . last Tuesday morning, three days ago.'

'So?'

'So we came to ask you about Walter Hughes. You can also tell us what your connection is with Margaret Percival.'

'I can?'

'If you like.'

'Suppose I don't want to?' Siddle stood in the doorway of his flat, which was in a low-rise, newbuild development on Water End, overlooking the shimmering Ouse as it wound through the green meadows of Clifton Ings.

'We will become suspicious,' Thompson Ventnor said.

'Very suspicious,' added Yellich, 'and you must know what policemen are like when they – when we – get suspicious.'

'Like a dog with a bone.'

'Like a hungry dog with a bone.'

'So what do you want to know?'

'Are we doing this standing here?' Yellich pressed. 'Or are you going to invite us in?'

'Alternatively we have a very comfortable interview room at the police station,' Ventnor added with a smile.

Siddle hesitated then said, 'Come in.' He turned and walked down the narrow entrance hallway. As he passed a room a female voice said, 'Who is it, Adrian?'

'Just a couple of guys. Stay in there.' He shut the door. He walked into the living room of his flat. 'You might have chosen a more appropriate time.'

'Well, we were not to know; but since we are here . . .'

Siddle sank into a canvas reclining chair and by a wave of his hand invited Yellich and Ventnor to take a seat. They sat in separate armchairs.

Yellich glanced around him and read the room. He read money – above all else, he read money: flat plasma-screen TV, top-of-the-range DVD recorder/player . . . a vinyl record player alongside a CD player . . . reeds of pampas grass in an earthenware jar by the window . . . polished wooden floorboards.

'You seem to be doing well for yourself,' Yellich remarked.

'I get by.'

'Still unemployed?'

Siddle smirked. 'As I said, I get by.'

'So where does the money come from? The money for this . . . this flat, these . . . these gadgets?'

'I get by.' Siddle was stone-faced. He wasn't giving anything away.

'Anything that would interest us?'

Siddle shrugged. 'Depends what you are interested in.'

'So, what's your connection with Walter Hughes?'

'Who?'

'Wally Hughes,' Ventnor snarled. 'Two-bullets-in-the-head Hughes – *that* Wally Hughes.'

'Don't know anyone of that name.'

'First lie.'Yellich smiled. 'You were in Armley together.'

'Bet you do a grand job of digging holes for yourself, eh, Adrian?'

'Oh, him?' Siddle glanced out of the window.

'Yes "him". You don't get views like that from inside . . . but you know that.'

'Having been there.' Ventnor smiled.

'So tell us what you know about Walter Hughes.'

'Just a guy . . . a young guy . . . had ambition.'

'So how well did you know him?'

'Gave him an intro to Margaret Percival. He was looking for work.'

'So what did he do for Mrs Percival?'

'This and that . . . He was a gofer.'

'So what did or did he not go for to earn two bullets in the head?'

Siddle shrugged. 'Haven't a clue.'

'Not giving much away, are you?' Ventnor sighed.

Again, another shrug.

'People with your attitude always seem to have something to hide – and we always find out what it is . . . eventually,' Yellich added. 'And you're a young man, plenty of time. So what do you do for Margaret Percival?'

'Drive her . . . She doesn't drive.'

'You drive her . . . and that little job pays for all this?' – Yellich indicated the plasma screen and the DVD player – 'and this flat? Are you buying or renting?'

'Buying.'

'What did you declare as your occupation to the building society?'

'Confidential.'

'Who's your mortgage with?'

'Again, confidential. How did you find me anyway?'

'You're in the system, Mr Siddle.'

'Still doesn't explain how you linked me with Wally Hughes's murder.' A note of menace crept into Siddle's voice. 'Somebody had to finger me.'

'Nobody fingered you.'

'Well, you would say that, wouldn't you? You'd do anything to protect your grasses.' He paused. 'That's it' – he stood – 'I want you out of here. Next time we talk it'll be on the record with a lawyer present.'

'All right.' Yellich stood. Ventnor did likewise.

'I like things to be done proper, like. Everything on the record.'

'So do we. So we'll be back.'

'You will?'

'Oh, we think so,' Ventnor snarled. 'This has been very informative.'

'I haven't told you anything.'

More than you know. You're definitely hiding something. I mean, you wouldn't know who might happen to own a black Mercedes S Class and also a bottle-green Range Rover?'

'You see, if we can find those cars and we find Wally Hughes's DNA inside either of them . . .' – Yellich smiled as he saw the colour drain from Siddle's face – 'well, then we are well on our way to cracking the case.'

'We'll see ourselves out.' Ventnor also smiled. 'Let you get back to your afternoon delight.'

That evening, Thompson Ventnor drove to the large, rambling ivy-covered house, which stood on the outskirts of York. He opened the front door, smiled at the nurse, who returned his smile, and signed in the visitors' register. He climbed the wide, carpeted staircase, which smelled of air-freshener and furniture polish, and entered a room where elderly people sat in chairs, where the television was permanently switched on. One elderly man showed an alertness and a joyful look of recognition as Ventnor entered the room, but by the time Ventnor had crossed the floor space between the door and the man the look of recognition had gone, replaced by a look of happiness, though there was no interaction between the elderly man and his surroundings.

Ventnor knelt before the man and said, 'Oh, my daddy . . . what's become of you?'

The man walked into the police station and asked to speak to Detective Chief Inspector Hennessey.

'Sorry, sir, he's gone home,' the duty constable said. 'Can I help?'

The man glanced at his watch: nine – quarter past nine. 'I didn't think it was as late as that.' His voice was slurred; he rocked unsteadily on his feet. 'I'll come back in the morning . . . walk down to the railway station, get a taxi home.' He smiled at the white-shirted constable. 'I don't think you'd want me to get behind the wheel of my car . . .'

'Don't think so either, sir. Can I take a message?'

'Yes . . . the name's Toby Murphy. Just say I'd like to work for myself. Mr Hennessey will know what it means.'

It was Friday, the sixth of June, 21.15 hours.

Seven

Saturday, 7 June, 09.30 hours – 16.32 hours
*in which the kind reader learns of Commander Sharkey's
fears and a foot soldier is interviewed.*

'That does seem to be the way of it, sir,' Hennessey
agreed. 'Second-hand car dealers have often proved
themselves a conduit to the underworld, even upmarket
operations like Toby Murphy's.'

'It'll be interesting to see what he has to say.' Commander
Sharkey brushed down his neatly trimmed moustache.
He was a short man for a police officer, always meticulously turned out, in Hennessey's experience and observation, whilst his desk top was similarly neat in its
'everything-in-its-place' exactness. Behind him, to his
left, was a framed photograph of a younger Sharkey in
the uniform of an officer in the Royal Hong Kong Police,
and to his right a second framed photograph of an even
younger Sharkey in the uniform of a junior officer in
the British Army. 'And the Percival murder won't go
away, you feel?'

'No, sir; we thought we'd have to shelve it when we
heard of the murder of young Walter Hughes, but Hughes
seems to be part of the Percival web.'

'And the Saffer murders – the husband and wife?'

'Saffer of Saffer Ink. Again, not forgotten; neither is

143

Tommy White, presently languishing as a guest of Her Majesty, and who may have been wrongfully convicted.'

'Oh . . . that will look bad – especially since the amount of money given to wrongfully convicted persons now looks set to be reduced, so as to increase the amount given in compensation to victims.'

'And a wrongfully convicted person is not a victim?'

'Oh, my sympathies entirely, George; let's try and get White out before the proposals become carved in stone . . . if he *is* innocent.'

'If indeed.'

'Well, George, two things really . . .'

'Yes, sir.' Hennessey's heart sank. 'Really, sir, I think I know what you are going to say. I am certain there is no corruption here at Micklegate Bar.'

Sharkey smiled a brief and a rare smile. 'I hope you are correct, George; I couldn't cope with that sort of revelation. I had it there . . .' He indicated the photograph of himself when in the RHKP. 'It wasn't the sort of corruption I fear. I just had to look the other way and a wad of notes would be in my drawer the following morning. That's how it worked. I wasn't there very long, but I was part of it and the contamination is permanent. My wife and I used the money I earned in Hong Kong to put a deposit on our home. It's in the bricks and mortar . . . the children will one day inherit it; their heritage will be poisoned and their children's heritage. Heavens, talk about the sins of the father . . . but if you are certain . . .'

'As certain as I can be, sir.' Hennessey smiled reassuringly. 'I am sure you have a clean nick.'

'Well, I find that gratifying . . . and the other thing. I know I have mentioned this to you before, George.'

'I don't want to retire from a desk, sir. I assure you, I am well on top . . . well able to cope. I left the Royal Navy by walking off a destroyer, not from behind a desk, and I'd like to retire from the police force by walking away from my office in the CID corridor.'

'I hear you, but the memory of poor old Johnny Taighe haunts me.'

'Your maths teacher at school, sir? I think you have mentioned him.'

'The one and the same . . . poor old chap: just when he should have been allowed to soft-pedal into a well-earned retirement, they piled on the pressure. He wasn't up to teaching upper-school maths, but that's what they made him do. He had a large red nose, so he was drinking heavily, and he smoked like a chimney . . . they were warning signs that none of the staff picked up on. I see that in hindsight, but his colleagues should have seen them for what they were: he was burned out.'

'Yes, sir, a tragedy indeed.' Hennessey glanced at the liver-spotted backs of his hands, the saggy flesh, the protruding veins. 'But I am fit to carry on – very ready, very willing, very able . . . getting on, as we all are, but still up to the job.'

'Well, as long as you are sure, George. Just tap on my door – there's plenty of good and useful work to be done. Police–community liaison and school-liaison officers – yours for the asking.'

Hennessey stood and held up his hand. 'No, no, sir, just leave me where I am. I won't let you down.'

Hennessey walked out of Sharkey's office and, with no little relief, returned to his own office and the ringing telephone therein. He picked it up. 'Hennessey.'

'Enquiry desk, sir; gentleman called Murphy – Mr Toby Murphy – to see you, sir.'

'It feels so much of a relief.' Toby Murphy swilled the coffee round the white plastic mug.

145

'Do you want legal representation?' Hennessey sat back in the chair in the interview room.

Toby Murphy shook his head. 'No, no, thanks. I did some hard drinking last night, more than I have done in a long time. Certainly would not have impressed my doctor, but with the hard drinking came the hard thinking. I might need protection; they have a way of opening up your mouth if you talk too much . . .'

'The Chelsea smile – yes, we know of it.'

'So you can protect me?'

Hennessey thought of Mule Mulligan in his not-so-safe safe house in Durham but said, 'Yes, we can protect you' – he paused – 'but that depends on how much information you can provide. It also doesn't guarantee you protection from prosecution if you have committed an offence – especially of a magnitude we can't ignore.'

'Understood.' Murphy sipped his coffee. 'They probably know I am here; they have eyes everywhere in this town.'

'They?'

'Percival's crew. I don't think I can give you any hard evidence.'

'Just tell me what you know – this is off the record. If you begin to compromise yourself, I will advise you . . . warn you.'

'Appreciated.' Murphy was dressed in a rugby shirt and jeans; gone also was the cheery confidence of the used-car salesman. Instead he fidgeted nervously.

'So . . . in your own words.'

'Well, to put it bluntly, I have been paying Percival protection money for years.'

'I see.'

'I'm proud of my business; there is a certain safety in buying a used car from me. A good car for a fair price and reasonable trade-in terms too. I started my business by borrowing money from my mother. Three Fords – ex-fleet cars, so they were high-mileage but they had been well maintained. Customers don't like high-mileage cars, but really the mileage doesn't matter; the issue is how well the car has been maintained.'

'I see.'

'So I bought them, gave them each a full service, valeted them and banked on three customers that wouldn't be put off by a high mileage if they could be assured that the vehicle had been well maintained . . . and I did – sold all three within a week. I was twenty-two and on my way and I was able to repay my mother the money, plus interest, within twelve months. The fact that the source of my wealth was a loan from my mother meant that I always shied away from the dodgy end of the motor trade, and it can be dodgy, as you no doubt know.'

'Oh yes.' Hennessey sipped his coffee. 'Oh my, yes.'

'It would have tainted her memory if her money had been used to open the door to dodgy dealings.'

'Good for you.'

'So I was, I believe, a rare and endangered species, namely a gentleman in the motor trade. I always tried to be ethically steadfast.'

'Again, good for you.'

'Well, success has its downside – it has its pitfalls – and one is that you become noticed by criminals. I dare say it's the same thinking that makes the homes of the wealthy attractive to burglars and not the homes of the poor; the criminals will go where the pickings are good.'

'Yes . . . so what happened?'

'I was visited by Percival's crew – his gofers; they came with a message one day: they wanted money, five hundred a month . . . it's more than that now. I refused, I threatened them with the police and they stood up and said

"OK", and as they left, they dropped a brown-paper enve-
lope on my desk.'

'Photographs?'

'Yes, how did you know?'

'Been round the block a few times, Mr Murphy. Nothing
is new any more.'

'I imagine . . . sorry . . . I don't wish to imply . . .'

'No worries.' Hennessey smiled. 'My pension has been
calling my name for some months now and I am looking
forward to retirement. I have grandchildren; I want to spend
more time with them.'

'Nice . . . Is your son or daughter in the police force?'

'One son – and no, he's a barrister. I am very proud of
him. I collar them and charge them and he fights tooth
and nail to get them acquitted. He works on the North-
Eastern Circuit . . . from Sheffield up to Newcastle, on this
side of the Pennines.'

'Oh, but of course.' Toby Murphy paused. 'I have children . . . two, still at school; they won't be high flyers like
your son. Tracy wants to be a nurse and Patrick – he's
fixed up to follow me into the used-car business. I had
hoped for more for them, but neither of them shine,
academically speaking. Still, I love them both very
much . . . teenagers now . . . fascinated by music I find . . .
tuneless . . . utterly incomprehensible, but I mention them
because that was what was in the envelopes – I mean, not
Tracy or Patrick, but photographs of them out of doors,
with their friends . . . and photographs of our house . . .
even of our motorboat in Hull Marina . . . and that night
my premises were torched – every car . . . every car . . .
forty vehicles. You might remember it?'

'Yes, I think I do.'

'Made quite a media splash; it was even mentioned on
the national news . . . A large fire is a good story . . .'

'Sadly.'

'Yes . . . every car had one of its windows smashed, petrol poured in and then a match.'

'A bit dangerous.'

'Well, the fire-investigation people said the cars were not ignited until all had been doused with petrol on the inside. Very methodical – must have been quite a gang of them, each with a task to do, because the car alarms were sounding. Folk who lived opposite were disturbed in their sleep and the police thought that from the time the first car window was smashed open to the time the first match was lighted and thrown in was about a minute so . . . smash a window in each of forty cars . . . pour petrol into the cars . . . light the first match. The police and fire people thought about ten men in the gang.'

'At least, I'd say. The smashing of the windows isn't difficult; the difficulty would have been carrying the petrol in forty separate containers.'

'Just plastic milk bottles, one pint ones – forty of those, fill them with petrol, unscrew the top and drop it in upside down. Not a lot of bulk, or weight, if it's divided up between gang members.'

'I see.'

'So my stock was scrap.'

'Did you tell the police about the visit from Percival's gofers?'

'No . . .' Murphy glanced down and shook his head slowly. 'The photographs of my family . . . these people use fire. Having my business torched is one thing, but having petrol poured through my letter box when my family may be in the house . . .'

'I can understand that.'

'So the insurance company paid out eventually, but not before we had to move into a council house on Tang Hall. I had to sell our house to pay debts, you see. That was a bad time for us. It didn't fully cover the loss, but I was able to carry on. They seemed to know what was happening. They said, "We'll pay out on this one occasion, but not again." They said, "If someone is putting the squeeze on you, just pay up."'

'They said that?'

'Yes. They said they see it all the time. They said if the amount wanted was manageable, just to pay it: "Just pass the cost on to your customers, increase the asking price on your cars" – that was their unofficial advice and that's what I did. Took me a few months to rebuild my stock, but when I was up and running again, Percival's men called, looking pleased with themselves. They knew that I would pay up.'

'When was this?'

'About seven years ago. My tribute has doubled in that time, and I have to direct my customers to Percival Financing.'

'So why speak now?'

'Because it didn't stop there . . . and it's time it did stop.'

Hennessey nodded. 'What else?'

'They came borrowing cars . . . That's when I knew I was really being squeezed by Percival. A couple of his boys would come and say "Mr Percival wants a car," "Mr Percival wants a couple of cars." Sometimes they came back with minor damage to the bodywork but often with blood all over the rear seat.'

'That's what happened with the Mercedes and the Range Rover?'

'Yes. The Range Rover just needed a clean on the outside, but the Merc . . . tell your people to look at the Mercedes . . . it had blood everywhere. I had it valeted but bits of blood will be there.'

'So Mr Percival – that is, Duncan Percival?'

'Never met him, but heard the name – yes, Duncan Percival.'

'And recently?'

'Recently?'

'Well, I ask because five years ago Duncan Percival was kicked into a permanent vegetative state, and died a few days ago.'

'Really?'

'Yes, really.'

'Well, that explains it.'

'Explains what?'

'For the last few years it has always been "Mrs Percival wants a car".'

'What!' Hennessey couldn't contain his surprise, but the surprise was short-lived because, as he had just said to Toby Murphy, nothing was new any more. 'That is interesting.'

'So I've been a victim. I've told you all I know . . . I won't make a statement . . . I won't give evidence.'

'Who removed the Merc from your business premises?'

'Young man – never seen him before. And his mate. Two guys.'

'Would you recognize them again?'

'I might. I would certainly recognize one – he was badly scarred down one cheek' – Murphy drew a finger back from the right corner of his mouth – 'he was in his early twenties.'

'More mouth openings?'

'Seems so, but this one . . . this wasn't the full Monty – just one cheek and only halfway back. More like a warning than the full consequence – that was the impression I had. He was second fiddle – stood behind the first guy, was very nervous; he had been pressed into service . . . again, just the impression I had.'

'So we need to find "Scarface",' Hennessey mused. 'Would you look at some photographs for me?'

Toby Murphy nodded. 'Anything to help, without actually giving evidence.'

'I will do what I can to accommodate you; but you could be compelled to give evidence.'

'I will need protection.'

'That can be offered . . . but . . .'

'But?'

'You might not need it.'

'You think?'

'Well, if we can put this lot away – Percival and her gang . . .'

'I will still feel unsafe.'

'We'll see where we get to . . . I'll go and get the family album.'

'That's him!' Toby Murphy jabbed the photograph decisively. He had found the photograph in the fourth of the six albums Hennessey had brought for him to look through, and had done so after nearly thirty minutes' careful scrutiny. The 'him' in question was a thin-faced man, with a pale, sunken, death-like complexion and mousy pale hair. The scar on his right cheek was evident.

'It's not just the scar' – Murphy sat back – 'it's the whole . . .' – he encircled his face with his hand – 'the whole . . . visage . . . the emaciation. I mean, put him in striped pyjamas behind barbed wire and he wouldn't look out of place.'

'Yes . . .' Hennessey looked at the photograph: a wounded-looking soul. He studied the image. 'He looks like a pressed man, someone who's out of his depth. He might appreciate a lifeline.' He took a note of the case number as printed underneath the photograph, which showed the youth facing half away from the camera, the photographer cleverly having asked the subject to incline his scarred cheek towards the lens. 'Seen him before?'

'A few times . . . never really took much notice of him; I always looked at the one who did the asking – well, the demanding really . . .'

'Care to look at some other photos?'

'If you like . . . but the guy's nickname is "Siddie".'

'Siddie?'

'Yes, as if his Christian name was Sydney.'

'Or as if his surname might by Siddle?'

'Could be . . . whatever; the first guy asked the young guy – the one you called Scarface – to drive the Mercedes. As he handed him the keys, the youth said, "OK, Siddie."'

'Right.' Hennessey stood. 'If you'd wait here, please – just one photograph for you to look at, not another set of albums . . .'

'That's him,' Toby Murphy said for the second time that morning, as Hennessey showed him a photograph of Adrian Siddle.

'A lot of borrowed names in this case, boss.' Yellich looked at the file. 'Started with an Apsley House and now we have a Scarface.'

'Aye . . .' Hennessey nodded. 'Mind you, he is hardly the Scarface of the Scarface Mob fame – no machine-gun-wielding gangster from the prohibition era he. More of a frightened mouse well out of his depth who had his cheek slit . . . gangland retribution for young Adam Palfrey.'

'Shall we bring him in, boss?'

'Yes.' Hennessey glanced at Yellich and then at Ventnor. 'Yes . . . go now. He's frightened – go in hard, go in heavy and by the book. Arrest him in connection with the murder of Walter Hughes; put him in a cell and leave him to sweat for an hour or two, then you and I, Yellich – we will interview him. So you'd better get a solicitor for him.' Hennessey glanced at his watch. 'We should be getting the results from Wetherby back anytime. Fresh case, they give it priority.' He paused. 'Once he's back here, I want you, Ventnor, to take a SOCO team and go over Palfrey's drum. You'll need a warrant, but he's linked to a murder – and he lives alone, according to his sheet, so obtaining a warrant will be straightforward.'

'When do you intend to interview Margaret Percival, sir?'

'Not until we have something to charge her with. She'll know we have visited Scafe and Siddle; she'll be getting frightened . . . We'll let her sweat for a while; with luck she might start running in circles. Right, go and huckle Palfrey.'

The twin cassettes in the tape recorder turned slowly; the red recording light glowed.

'The time is fifteen thirty-six hours, the place Interview Room Three at Micklegate Bar Police Station, York; the date is Saturday the seventh of June. I am Detective Chief Inspector Hennessey. I am now going to ask the other persons present to identify themselves.'

'Detective Sergeant Yellich.'

'Bernice Nieto, of Ellis, Burden, Woodland and Lake, solicitors of St Leonard's Place, York, representing Mr Palfrey under the terms of the Police and Criminal Evidence Act 1985.'

'Palfrey, Adam . . . Adam Palfrey, and I didn't do anything.'

'All in good time, Adam. You don't mind if I call you Adam?'

Palfrey shook his head, 'No. Adam is OK.'

'So . . . I know you know why you are here.'

'Yes, but I didn't do nothing.'

'Well that's sensible – "Cough to nowt" is good advice, a good policy to observe – makes our job more difficult, but it's a bit of a two-edged sword. You see, if you persist in protesting your innocence and we ultimately can prove you're guilty, you invite a harsher sentence.'

'Specifics, please, Chief Inspector.' Bernice Nieto was a small, dark-haired woman, dressed in a grey two-piece suit, with an expensive watch. Hennessey thought her to be in her late twenties. The diamond in her engagement ring was, he further thought, the largest he had seen – far, far larger than he had been able to afford all those summers ago when he and Jennifer had got engaged. Her watch was also top of the range. She was a woman who was used to having money and Hennessey guessed that she didn't do a lot of Legal Aid work. Representing Adam Palfrey and those of his ilk was most probably something she did between the conveyancing of large and expensive properties. 'Let's please keep to the facts. Murder is a very serious crime.'

'Doesn't get more serious.' Hennessey leaned back in his chair. 'In fact it's quite a leap for you, Adam.' Hennessey looked at Palfrey, who averted his gaze. 'Had a glance at your track before I came here; that's why you were kept so long.'

'How long has my client been here?' Bernice Nieto looked at Hennessey over the rims of a pair of gold-framed spectacles.

'About four hours.'

'About is not good enough!'

'Sergeant Yellich?' Hennessey appealed to Yellich.

'Mr Palfrey has been here,' he said, consulting his watch, 'for exactly four hours and thirty-five minutes . . .'

'Four hours and thirty-five minutes!' Bernice Nieto gasped. 'You are sure of your ground, Chief Inspector – or getting careless. You realize that you have just one hour and twenty-five minutes to charge my client or release him?'

'Yes.' Hennessey smiled. 'I know that.' He then turned to Palfrey. 'You're petty.'

'Petty?' Palfrey glanced at him.

'Small-time . . . shoplifting . . .'

'I was hungry.'

'Possession of a controlled substance?'

'Cannabis – just enough to make a joint.'

'Receiving of stolen goods.'

'A box of pork chops someone had half-inched from the supermarket. I paid half the advertised price . . . it's tough on the dole.'

'So how did you find life on the inside?'

'I survived.'

'Possession with intent to supply . . . Fancy life as a premier-league drug dealer – ruining lives?'

Palfrey shook his head. 'I wasn't supplying anyone . . . anything. It's just the amount I had – about the size of three or four lumps of sugar. I wasn't going to supply anyone. It was for me.'

'It is a low threshold, I concede; but it still got you six out of twelve in Armley. Is that gaol as overcrowded as they say?'

'Four to a cell.'

'But you did your bird. How long were you in there for?'

'Four months . . . all that summer. It was raining when I went in the gates and raining when I came back out, and all the folk were talking about what a lovely summer they'd just had. I spent the time breathing in the smell of unwashed bodies. I didn't smell it after a while, but . . . a few hundred prisoners, a wet summer and just one shower a week . . . the screws on duty turned green. That was funny, but the visitors in the visitors' room were gagging for fresh air. I felt sorry for them.'

'A man with a heart.' Hennessey raised his eyebrows 'Well done you.'

Bernice Nieto did not interrupt but glanced at her watch from time to time.

156

'So you came out; you have prison time on your CV.'

'CV?'

'Well, let's just say you have done bird, got some prison time under your belt, ready for the big league – top division – and go to work for Percival.'

'How did you know?'

'We have sources.' Hennessey paused. 'Is that where you got that from?' He put his hand up to his cheek.

Palfrey put his fingertips to the scar on his cheek and shrugged.

'Open your mouth, did you?'

'Possibly.'

'Certainly, I'd say . . . but it couldn't have been a major infraction. I mean, otherwise it would have been both cheeks and not just halfway in but all the way to the corners of your mouth.'

'Even then it couldn't have been comfortable,' Yellich offered. 'In fact it couldn't have been comfortable at all.'

Palfrey shrugged. 'Yeah . . . it was uncomfortable.'

'Bled a lot?'

'Blood everywhere – walked into the hospital bleeding everywhere. One of the nurses had to sit down before she fell down. Thirty stitches I needed and they wouldn't give me anaesthetic. Can you imagine: pushing that needle in and out of my cheek with no painkiller.'

'That's what medics do; pain killers are for victims, not people who put unnecessary strain on the Health Service by avoidable injuries.'

'It wasn't avoidable.'

'Gangland – it was avoidable. You shouldn't have got mixed up with them in the first place. Shall we have some refreshment?'

'Refreshment!' Palfrey glanced at Hennessey.

'Well, we kept you waiting for so long – I do apologize for that . . . but some coffee or tea . . . from the vending machine, I'm afraid . . . real ersatz stuff . . .. tastes awful.'

When Adam Palfrey and Bernice Nieto were drinking coffee out of thin plastic mugs, Hennessey and Yellich stood beside the vending machine, also sipping very hot but utterly tasteless liquid.

'You're running out of time, skipper' – Yellich looked at his watch – 'less than an hour and we have to let him go.'

'I know.' Hennessey smiled.

'He'll run straight to the Percival female and tell her what we know.'

'Oh, I do hope so' – Hennessey sipped his coffee – 'I do hope so.'

When the interview had resumed, the tape recorder having been switched on, the time and date established, the persons present once again having identified themselves, Hennessey said, 'We have a witness, Adam.'

'Yes, a member of the public saw the cars driving away after abducting Walter Hughes,' Yellich added.

'A Range Rover and a Mercedes S Class.'

'This is Yorkshire, the City of York; there's a lot of money in the farming areas round the city; Range Rovers are not uncommon,' Yellich explained, 'but Mercedes S Class – they are a bit rarer. Asked our computer to list all locally registered black S Class. There was . . . well, guess how many black Mercedes S Class are registered in York.'

Palfrey shrugged his shoulders. 'How many?'

Yellich held up his index finger.

'One . . .' Palfrey gasped.

'You should have used a Volkswagen,' Hennessey explained; 'that would really have stopped little us.'

'But one S Class, registered to a used-car dealership . . . and not only was it there on the forecourt, gleaming in the sun under all those tiny plastic flags of many colours . . .

but . . . but bang next door to it was a bottle-green Range Rover.'

'Had to be the Range Rover we were seeking,' Yellich explained. 'See how we picked up the trail?'

'So nobody grassed you up,' Hennessey added; 'nobody needs their cheeks opening. So we impounded the two cars – took them to Wetherby.'

'Wetherby?'

'That's where our forensic-science laboratory is. They're going over them now. They were very clean, the cars, very clean – inside and out.'

'But not clean enough,' Yellich added. 'Inside the Merc was one of your fingerprints.'

'Not even one,' Hennessey said. 'A partial . . .'

'Yes, sorry' – Yellich inclined his head towards Hennessey – 'a partial . . . but it's enough.'

'It puts you inside that car. That's a very classy, classy motor for a lad on income support to be inside . . .'

'There's also blood inside the car – a few specks.'

'That blood has still to be identified, but if it turns out to be Walter Hughes's blood, then you have a lot of explaining to do.'

'Six months in Armley.' Yellich shook his head. 'You can do that on your back. But a life stretch in Durham – that is different.'

'Very different,' Hennessey added.

'You have no evidence against my client.' Bernice Nieto slapped her palm on the table. 'What is he doing here?'

'Helping with inquiries.'

'But you've arrested him!'

'Yes – and we are searching his flat.'

'My flat!' Palfrey glared at Hennessey.

'Yes, your flat. Are we going to find anything of interest?'

'I'm not saying nothing.' Palfrey looked at the table top.

'Well, that's your choice . . . but you can help yourself, instead of helping Margaret Percival.'

Palfrey looked at Hennessey.

'Oh yes, we know you work for her; we know she took over the business when her husband was kicked into a vegetative state, and she hasn't done you any favours by putting you inside a top-of-the-range motor with Walter Hughes bleeding everywhere. She should have used a stolen VW and then torched it. That would have put you in the clear.'

'But she, or her lieutenants, have dropped you in it.'

The already pale Palfrey paled even further.

'Are you going to live up to your name?'

'My name? Adam?'

'No . . .' Hennessey shook his head. 'I was thinking of Palfrey. Do you know what a palfrey is?'

Adam Palfrey shook his head.

'It's a packhorse . . . or a saddle horse. A bit like a mule.'

'A mule?'

'Yes . . . so are you going to be a mule? Carry the can while Percival gets away with it?'

'I just did what I was told.'

'Ah . . .' Bernice Nieto raised a finger in warning. 'Careful what you say, Mr Hennessey. My client's last remark is of no consequence; he could have been referring to anything – anything at all. It is not specific enough to incriminate him.'

'All right.' Hennessey held up his hand. 'We'll do this by the book.' He looked at Palfrey, 'We can offer protection . . .'

'Like you protected Mule Mulligan – speak of mules – like you protected him?'

'How do you know about that? Were you there?' Hennessey leaned forward.

Palfrey nodded his head.

'For the record, please.'

Palfrey shook his head and smiled 'For the record,' he said and then shook his head again.

'Did you have any part in it?'

Palfrey shook his head.

'But you witnessed it?'

Palfrey nodded his head.

'Did you know what was going to happen?'

Another shake of his head.

'I see . . . so you witnessed it and what you witnessed came as a shock?'

Palfrey nodded.

'Again, I see . . . I see . . .' Hennessey leaned back in his chair. 'So was it the case that you were driven to Mulligan's house, witnessed his murder, and on the way back someone said, "That's what you get if you talk, and the police can't keep you safe for ever?"'

'More or less.' Palfrey nodded. 'More or less.'

'Mule Mulligan was exposed by a mistake on our part. Most times folk stay hidden.'

'Most times?'

'All other times that I have known, it has been successful.'

'So what happens now?' Palfrey asked.

'Well, that is up to you.'

'Meaning?'

'Well, that depends what you do . . . and how safe you feel.'

'Safe?'

'Yes, safe. This is a heavy crew you're involved in; they will know you have been lifted. We've got nothing to hold you on – not until the blood in the Mercedes is confirmed as being that of Walter Hughes. Then we will rearrest you. It will be Hughes's blood, won't it?'

Palfrey shrugged. 'No comment.'

'Which is tantamount to saying yes.'

'It's tantamount to saying nothing,' Bernice Nieto snapped. 'It's a non-incriminating reply. No comment means no comment.'

'Very well . . . but we have to play by rules which protect you, Adam; Percival plays by rules which protect her.'

'So? Meaning?'

'Well, meaning that you were allowed to witness the murder of Mule Mulligan and then allowed a small part in the murder of Walter Hughes, as an initiation into the Percival gang. Is that what was happening – you were a foot soldier getting promoted?'

Palfrey shrugged his shoulders.

'I'll take that as a yes.'

'You'll take it as nothing, Chief Inspector.' Nieto's voice was firm, hard, final.

'So you've coughed.'

'No, I haven't.'

'They don't know that.' Hennessey smiled. 'You know, Adam, I will be honest with you. I brought you in here to frighten you.'

'You succeeded.'

'This is premier-division . . . this is big-league . . . this is hardball. You're not looking at a short sentence – not this time.'

'Yes, you said.'

'You'll be in your mid-thirties by the time you get out of gaol. Anyway, I was hoping you'd go straight to Percival or whoever you took orders from, tell them what we know. They would then start to panic, and we'd knock 'em over like skittles. That was the plan – sweep you up with them.'

'Hardly ethical, Chief Inspector.' Once again, Bernice Nieto glanced at Hennessey over the rim of her spectacles.

'Well, that was the plan, but now I think I'd be putting your life at risk.'

'My life? I haven't told you anything . . .'

'They don't know that and they will be frightened of what you could tell us. They'll do anything to stop you testifying. Anything.'

Adam Palfrey sagged.

'It's not safe for you out there now,' Yellich added.

'You said protection works?'

'Yes; Mule Mulligan was unlucky. He also should have lived in a big city – Durham is too small to hide in.'

'What does it mean, police protection?'

'New name, new identity – I mean, officially new ID – new National Insurance number. Adam Palfrey disappears. Do you have anyone? Any family?'

'No . . . no one. My father . . . never knew my father; he was a sailor when my mother used to live in Hull. He came off a boat, sired me, went back on the boat. My mother brought me up. She died a few years ago . . . so no one – just me.'

'You're lucky, then; you can make a clean break. Most people have someone; that makes it difficult to hide completely. But you can vanish.'

'How does it work?'

'You walk into a room . . . by yourself. A police officer who does not know you and will never see you again allows you to look at a list of names, and you choose one. Then you can choose where you want to live.'

'Anywhere?'

'Anywhere in the UK. Clean start. You're a young guy – not unintelligent . . . You could get into adult education.'

'I've always fancied the south coast . . . Brighton . . . Bournemouth . . .'

'Anywhere you like, but nowhere small; you have to hide.'

'I'll grow a beard.'

'Ideal. You've got long hair; I'd cut it if I were you.'

'Yeah.' Palfrey smiled. 'A new start . . . I'll stay clear of crime.'

'And in return?' Bernice Nieto asked.

'Well, depending upon the extent of your client's involvement in the murder of Walter Hughes and Mule Mulligan . . . we may drop charges.'

'May?'

'Yes, may – depending on his involvement. The more on the edge, the more likely we'll drop charges. The rough rule of thumb we apply is: if the crime took place without your client's active participation, or some small degree of participation, we will not bring charges. Can't offer this deal to the person who dealt the death blow.'

'Yes, but in return,' Bernice Nieto pressed, 'in return . . . in return . . .'

'A statement from your client implicating the prime movers . . . and his willingness to testify.'

There was a gentle tap on the interview-room door.

'The time is sixteen fourteen hours.' Hennessey reached for the tape-recorder on/off switch. 'I am halting the interview in response to a knock on the door.' He switched the machine off, stood, walked to the door, opened it and left the room.

Thompson Ventnor raised his eyebrows as Hennessey stepped into the corridor. 'Some boy this, boss.'

'What do you mean?'

'How old is he? – twenty, twenty-two?'

'About that.'

'With one of the plushest drums in York.'

'Really?'

'I knew where the address was – out in the sticks; thought I'd be going to a cottage . . .'

'And?'

'A very big house, a very big house indeed: indoor swimming pool, Ferrari in the garage, two young women who said they were "Adam's housekeepers".'

'More than meets . . .'

'Yes, boss, much more. The house itself is clean – nothing to implicate him in anything.'

'OK. Check with Land Registry; find out who owns that property.'

'I'm on it, boss, but it won't be open until Monday now.'

Hennessey returned to the interview room. He switched on the tape recorder and said, 'DCI Hennessey has re-entered the room; the interview is recommenced at sixteen sixteen hours. That was my sergeant, Adam – just been to your drum. You'll be pleased to know that we found nothing incriminating.'

Palfrey smiled.

'But not what we expected – your home, I mean: a large house in the country . . . a Ferrari in the garage.'

Bernice Nieto glanced at Palfrey, then at Hennessey. 'Mr Palfrey, Legal Aid doesn't pay at all; it is only for those persons who cannot afford a lawyer. If you have means, you must pay for your representation.'

'Came as a surprise to us, ma'am,' Hennessey explained. 'That's why we called you: you are the duty Legal Aid solicitor.'

'Yes.' She drummed her fingers on the desk. 'I will remain for the rest of the interview, but if Mr Palfrey has such wealth as you have just indicated, then he will have to pay for his own legal defence.'

'So what's the story, Adam? No visible means of support and you live in a house like that, with a car like that in the garage.'

'I just get to live there; I don't own it.'

'Who does?'

Palfrey remained silent.

'We'll find out; my sergeant's going to check with the Land Registry.'

'Mrs Percival,' Adam Palfrey sniffed, '– it belongs to

165

her. I sort of watch it for her; it needs to be lived in to keep the burglars out.'

Hennessey smiled. 'That's rich: the criminal afraid of other criminals . . . so . . . you are house-sitting it?'

'Yeah . . . could say.'

'All right, so do you want to tell us what happened to Walter Hughes?'

'He was skimming.'

'Skimming?'

'Had his hand in the till.'

'Whose till?'

'Dunno . . . Presume it was Mrs Percival's. They were working for her . . .'

'They?'

'Siddle and Scafe . . . They did the business on Walter – them and me and some other boys.'

'Other boys?'

'There was a mob. Don't know all the names. Bundled Hughes into the Merc and drove off, took him from his house in Osbaldwick . . . little flat. Took him out, kept him for a couple of days but he wouldn't say where he had put the money. Siddle shot him, twice . . . almost point-blank.'

'You sure it was Siddle?'

'Positive. I was standing next to him. Siddle had the gun; Siddle fired the shots – bang, bang.'

'And Scafe was there too?'

'Yes, they were like boss one and boss two; the rest were just soldiers.'

'And Margaret Percival's involvement?'

'You'll have to ask her that.'

'Oh, we will, we will. All right, we'd better get this down in the form of a statement.'

'Then I get to go to Bournemouth?'

'Not as fast as that, but you're on your way.'

Yellich looked at Palfrey and thought that he had seen him before, some time in the recent past and in connection with this inquiry . . . somewhere . . . somewhere.

It was Saturday, the seventh of June, 16.32 hours.

Eight

Monday, 9 June, 10.15 hours – 14.32 hours
*in which a house of cards falls and a middle-aged couple
enjoy an early night.*

'**K** ind of you.' Scafe smiled.

'Kind?' Hennessey repeated. 'What do you mean?'

'Oh . . . to let me enjoy the weekend. I mean if you'd really wanted to be spiteful, you would have huckled me on Saturday evening – based on what the youth told you.'

'Police officers like weekends too . . . and you weren't going anywhere.'

'And you let me sweat a bit.'

'Possibly . . . possibly that was part of it.'

'I'd say it was a huge part.' Scafe smiled. 'I know how you operate.' Scafe had a hard face, Hennessey thought, a con's face – cold eyes. He also wore a smug 'you can't touch me' expression.

'Let's just say that we were in no hurry.'

'You've got Siddle and Margaret Percival in here too?'

Hennessey glanced round the interview room: the red glow of the recording light of the tape recorder; Yellich silent yet steadfast by his side; the solemn and serious elderly solicitor who had introduced himself as Bentham and who was also part of the Ellis, Burden, Woodland and Lake firm of solicitors for whom Bernice Nieto worked. It was, in fairness, a huge practice, which did a

168

lot of criminal work, much of it low-paying Legal Aid work. 'Yes, yes we have.'

'So, who coughs first gets the best deal?'

'Well, as I have told you – the first cough has been made; Adam Palfrey's got his deal.'

'He's made his statement – implicating me?'

'And Siddle and a few others.'

'Silly boy . . .'

'Why? Because he's a dead man – is that your code? Grass and you die, after having your mouth opened a little bit? Is that what you plan for him?'

'Well, he did open his mouth, but that's not why he's been silly.'

'No?'

'No . . .'

'Tell me.'

'He has been silly because he assumed you wouldn't check his story.'

Hennessey remained silent. He stared intently at Scafe, who continued to look smug.

'There's got to be something in it for me.'

'Has there? We do not plea-bargain. Our cousins on the other side of the Atlantic do that; we don't. Our judges set the penalty, not Crown Prosecution Service lawyers. All we can do is ask you to turn Queen's evidence; won't wholly exonerate you, but it will be reflected in your sentence.'

'I am guilty of conspiracy to murder: my sentence is life.'

'Mr Scafe, I would caution you.' Bentham spoke with a deep voice.

'Well, I mean, I am guilty according to Palfrey . . . but only according to Palfrey.'

'Are you saying he lied to us?'

'Oh, yes' – Scafe smiled – 'from beginning to end. The

169

only truthful thing he has told you is that he wants out. That is true: he wants to make a new start. All of us think like that at some point or other, but it's not so simple – you can't leave a gang like ours; you're a loose cannon . . . you know where too many bodies are buried. The only thing to do with a loose cannon is silence it for the good of the crew. So I want to cut a deal for myself.'

'Well, no plea bargain, like I said, but talk.'

'I've been round the block a few times . . .'

'We know; I spoke to the Greater Manchester Police. They were interested to know that you had fetched up this side of the mountains.'

'I bet they were: I have to keep one step ahead of them; but this crew' – he nodded his head with no small degree of contempt in the direction of the other interview rooms – 'they are not going to take me down with them . . . like, no way. I want out.'

'So, talk to me.'

'You arrested Palfrey from his house?'

'Yes.'

'Big house – too big for a boy of his age.'

'That's what we thought; we're checking the Land Registry now.'

'Should have told me; I could have saved you a job. His mother owns it – installed him in it with his "housekeepers", I believe they are called. Every boy needs his comforts – his home comforts . . . if you see what I mean.'

'Yes, I get the gist. But his mother – is she a lottery winner? He said she had died.'

'No. She's Margaret Percival. And she's very much alive.'

The silence in the room was nearly audible, broken only by a gasp from Yellich.

Scafe looked pleased with himself. 'Thought that would surprise you . . . but you'd have found out eventually; as soon as you got to the Land Registry you would have found out.'

'So what happened to Walter Hughes? Adam Palfrey said he was murdered by Siddle for skimming.'

'Half right: he was murdered for skimming, but by Adam Palfrey. Adam Palfrey was the trigger man – kept him alive for two days . . . at his house.'

'Palfrey?'

'Palfrey. He's the boss – well, the boss's son. That makes him number two; though he still wants out. So he's grassing all he can to get witness protection.'

'He said *you* were the boss, after Margaret Percival.'

'Well, as Christine Keeler once said, "He would, wouldn't he?"'

'You are implicating yourself, Mr Scafe.' Again Bentham cautioned him in a deep, almost menacing voice.

Scafe turned to him. 'Well, what else can I do? Once grassing starts, all you can do is grass back – try to work out the best deal for yourself. Besides which, grassing on a grass is OK.'

'OK?' Bentham queried.

'Allowed. I won't get rolled in the showers for grassing a grass.'

'I see.' Bentham raised an eyebrow. 'How interesting . . . but mostly I do conveyancing, you see . . .'

'So, Palfrey shot Hughes?'

'Yes. The gun is in the Ouse. You won't find it now – a long way downstream. Well out of York; nearer Selby than York. Couldn't find the exact spot; it was dark, in the sticks . . . It's well gone.'

'All right.'

'What was your part on the night?'

'Wheelman . . . under duress. Palfrey had the gun on me.'

'I want you to take that into account, Chief Inspector,'

Bentham said solemnly; 'my client acted under duress. This is amounting to a full confession and I want that taken into account: under duress; and just the driver.'

'Yes.' Hennessey spoke half-heartedly. 'Yes . . . yes . . . so what is Margaret Percival's source of income?'

'Extortion, so far as I can tell – protection money. You'll need to talk to Siddle about that; he's the bookkeeper . . . as well as . . . well . . .' Scafe shrugged.

'As well as what?'

'As well as being her "toy boy", as I understand the expression to be. She has bought him a lovely BMW.'

'Scafe said that about me?' Siddle gasped. 'Don't he know the rules?'

'Grassing up a grass is not grassing. Apparently.' Hennessey shrugged. 'So I have just learned.'

'He's doing a deal for himself?'

'Yes.' Hennessey nodded. 'So is Adam Palfrey.'

Siddle paled. 'Palfrey as well?'

'Yes, Palfrey as well. New name, new start in the soft South of England.'

'He's got that?'

'He thinks he has.' Hennessey leaned back in his chair and glanced at the solicitor who was representing Adrian Siddle: short, demure, studious-looking. She'd introduced herself as Ruth Elliot, of March, Wrigley & Co. 'But that looks like it's going to be rescinded.'

Siddle took a deep breath and looked sideways. 'What has Scafe got from this?'

'An early parole. He said that there was a gun to his head, so he might even escape a charge of conspiracy to murder – never know.'

Siddle remained silent for a few minutes and then turned to Ruth Elliot. 'What can I do? I'm being thrown to the wolves.'

'Can my client and I have a few moments alone, please? We'd like to discuss his options?'

'Of course.' Hennessey stood; Yellich did likewise. He said, 'The interview is suspended at eleven twenty hours to allow Ms Elliot and Mr Siddle to confer in private.' He switched off the tape recorder and he and Yellich left the room.

'Falling like a house of cards,' Yellich said, as he and Hennessey stood by the coffee-vending machine once more, sipping hot and tasteless liquid from white plastic beakers.

'Yes – nice, isn't it? We'll put them all in the dock and let them condemn each other. Ah . . .' Hennessey glanced to his left as Thompson Ventnor approached, holding a notebook in his hand and looking pleased with himself. 'Margaret Percival.' Hennessey smiled. 'She's the owner of Palfrey's house.'

'Yes.' Ventnor looked crestfallen. 'How . . .?'

'David Scafe told us – could have saved you a journey. Sorry, we didn't expect them to capitulate so quickly and easily.'

'All anxious to do deals at the expense of the others,' Yellich added. 'Adam Palfrey is Margaret Percival's son, he explained.'

'Her son!'

'Yes. Came as a surprise to us,' Yellich added.

'Well . . .' Ventnor looked deflated. 'And all this came out because a vegetable died . . .'

'And a young man stopped two bullets with his skull.' He dropped his half-empty beaker into the metal waste-paper bin. 'Don't forget young Wally Hughes's eclipsed life. Dreadful penalty to pay for theft; but then, he was a volunteer – nobody presses you into the service of organized crime. So . . . let's go back and see what sort of offer Mr Siddle wants to make.'

'My client wishes to make a full confession,' Ruth Elliot announced, after the preliminaries of introductions had been made for the benefit of the tape recorder, 'on the understanding that his cooperation will be noted and taken into account.'

'Agreed.' Hennessey leaned forward. 'So tell us, Adrian—'

'It would be easier if you would ask me questions; I don't know where to start.'

'Well . . . We understood from Scafe that you are Margaret Percival's bookkeeper?'

'Yes.'

'So she keeps records?'

'Of . . . ?'

'People . . . businesses that pay her protection money?'

'Where are these records?'

'In her house . . . in her study . . . on her computer. She never thought she'd get busted.'

'Few do.'

'Details of other businesses?'

'Such as?'

'Massage parlours . . . in York . . . Leeds . . . Sheffield.'

'Immoral earnings.'

'Worse.'

'Meaning?'

'East European women – kept under duress.'

'People-trafficking? Sexual slavery?'

Adrian Siddle nodded. 'I wasn't happy with that. Mainly it was her and her son – Palfrey.'

'What are the addresses of these establishments, do you know?'

Siddle knew – recounted them as Hennessey wrote the details on his pad. He tore the page off and handed it to Yellich. 'I want the York address raided now.'

'Yes, sir.'

'Before you do that, pass the other addresses on to the West and South Yorkshire forces.'

'Yes, sir.' Yellich stood.

'The time is eleven forty-seven hours; Detective Sergeant Yellich has left the room. Any other ventures?'

'No. That's it: extortion and vice.'

'And murder. What do you know about the murders?'

'Pretty well everything. I've been with the family for a few years. Would you believe me when I tell you what a relief this feels? You drift into this lifestyle . . . this job; but once in, getting out is next to impossible.'

'So I believe.' Hennessey paused. 'So what happened to Margaret Percival's husband?'

'He got a good kicking.'

'Oh, we know that, but why and who?'

'Why? Why? Because of what he did to Adam Palfrey.'

'What did he do?'

Adrian Siddle ran his finger across his cheek. 'The scar.'

'Percival did that?'

'Yes. Adam Palfrey and Duncan Percival never hit it off. Adam's illegitimate . . . he was part of the package when Margaret Palfrey became Margaret Percival. Bit of a mother's boy was Adam, turned him into a vicious little thug. Anyway, Adam started bad-mouthing Duncan so Duncan taught him a lesson. Didn't give him the full smile, just a "wee grin", as he put it.'

'I see.'

'That didn't go down too well with Margaret.'

'It wouldn't.'

'Anyway, she was well into the business by then; she was ready to put in a power bid, and what Duncan did to Adam was the nudge she needed. So she put a team together – told them where he'd be without any minders . . .'

'The holiday cottage.'

Adrian Siddle nodded. 'They kept that a secret – the

address I mean – made sure they were never followed when they went there. Anyway, Margaret drove off, leaving Duncan alone for half an hour. The boys didn't quite do the job they were supposed to do, but near enough, so they got paid.'

'Who were those men?'

'Illegals from Eastern Europe. Margaret paid them well, allowed them to stay submerged for a month after that. Anyway, the fact that they didn't kill him turned out to be useful. She kept him alive so she could play the grieving widow; suspicion never fell on her because of that. Not that she did anything for him – had a nurse come in and do all that. She never set eyes on him for months at a time.'

'And you were her lover?'

'Yes.' Siddle nodded. 'It was quite pleasant for a time . . . Then you realize you are trapped. Not so pleasant then, despite the silk sheets and king-size four-poster bed.'

'So, the Saffers?'

'Decoys – they were murdered as decoys. The police were sniffing round, looking for the guys who attacked Duncan and turned him into a vegetable. Margaret said they needed a higher-profile crime to investigate – stretch their resources. So she gave them one. They had a dispute with the Saffers over a building . . .'

'Who blew them away?'

'Adam Palfrey – just walked up to their house with a shotgun. He's a killing machine . . . he's not human.'

'Tommy White?'

'Fitted him up – put the shotgun in his lock-up and made an anonymous call to the police. Put some stuff from the Saffers' home in there as well – jewellery, to make it look like a burglary murder.'

'Were you involved?'

'Wheelman . . .'

'Another wheelman. Nobody's ever more than a wheelman in this case . . . with a gun to his head.'

'It's the truth.'

'Mule Mulligan up there in Durham in police protection?'

Siddle nodded. 'Well, Margaret had no love for her husband but Mule had turned Queen's. She had eyes on . . . well, on this building – followed plain-clothes officers who left in twos and in cars; kept trailing the car if it left York. Then one car went a long way up the A1 . . . and . . .'

'Who did that to Mule Mulligan?'

'Palfrey and Scafe.'

'And you were the wheelman?'

'No. On that job they drove. Once the police had been tailed to that address in Durham, they went up later that day . . . well, at night.'

'How many people work for Margaret Percival?'

Siddle shrugged. 'Thirty – that's counting the staff in the massage parlours.'

'Are there records?'

'Yes. All in her office and on her computer.'

'You'll be providing us with the password?'

Siddle nodded. 'Actually, you don't need it: your computer wizards can get into any system without knowing the password; but I'll let you have it anyway . . . save about five minutes of police time. It's "black widow" – not very original but that's it.'

'Black widow.' Hennessey scribbled on his pad. 'And Walter Hughes?'

'Palfrey shot him. I drove the other car.'

'Wheelman.' Hennessey sighed.

'So this will help me?' Siddle appealed. 'I mean, I have to start working for myself now. Thieves' honour is out of the window. Everybody is working for themselves. I've done time; I can do it again. But as short as possible.'

'That's the correct attitude,' Hennessey replied. 'You start to work towards your parole now. We'll need a signed statement.'

'Of course.'

'You know' – Ruth Elliot closed her notepad and put her ballpoint in her handbag – 'I don't think my services are further required.'

Hennessey returned from the charge bar to the interview room, where Yellich was reading over Adrian Siddle's statement.

'We chat with the black widow now, skipper?' Yellich glanced up as Hennessey entered the room.

'No.' Hennessey sat in the chair recently vacated by Siddle.

'No?' Yellich was surprised.

'No. I think we charge her with something – something that will get her remanded. Living off immoral earnings won't get her a remand . . .'

'People-trafficking? Sexual slavery?'

'Yes, that will do – so she's looking at four or five years . . . Then we'll go and visit her in the women's prison in a week's time and chat to her about murder . . . two counts. Doubtless she'll give up all she knows about Scafe and Siddle, maybe even her own son. She's ruthless enough.'

'She'll fall furthest,' Yellich mused, '– from that house to a cell in Newhall. How the mighty fall.'

'She'll do about fifteen years with remission – won't come out to much. Under the asset-seizure rules, she can keep only what she can prove was purchased with legitimately earned money. Did they raid the massage parlour?'

'Yes, boss – three Romanian men in custody, fifteen East European women being interviewed by the immigration people.'

'Fifteen!'

'Yes: four in the parlour, the others resting in an adjacent house ready to start the evening and night shift. Haven't checked with the Land Registry to see who owns the parlour or the house; but my money is on Margaret Percival.'

It was Monday, 9 June, 14.32 hours.

'In the end, all we could get was guilty to conspiracy to murder in respect of the death of Walter Hughes – no proof that Palfrey did it. He said he didn't; Siddle and Scafe said he did. But they were all present, and all took part in the abduction. They collected the mandatory life sentence.' Hennessey sipped his soup and glanced out of the rain-lashed restaurant window at the leafless trees and thought that winter had come early that year. 'Palfrey went NG, as my son would say, to the murder of Donald Percival, but the jury found against him – powerful motive and Scafe's testimony. He was also found guilty of murdering the Saffers . . . They were very, very innocent victims.'

'Yes' – his dining companion placed her spoon in the soup bowl – 'I followed the case in the *Yorkshire Post*.'

'They just condemned each other. Palfrey got four life sentences. Of all of them, he'll serve the longest sentence.'

'Twenty-five years, minimum tariff, I read.'

'Yes, and the judge is not thought of as a harsh sentencer. For him to set a minimum of twenty-five years . . . He took a very dim view of the antics of Adam Palfrey.'

'Margaret Percival collected twenty years for four counts of conspiracy to murder . . . Seems fair.'

'Yes. She really was behind the murders of her husband, the Saffers, Walter Hughes and Mule Mulligan, but the jury couldn't decide on the Mulligan murder, so she was acquitted on that count.'

'So I read.' The woman smiled warmly. 'Are you going to seize her assets?'

'All we can. She won't come out to much. Single person's flat and the dole. Tommy White's had his conviction quashed. He's full of anger and resentment, but he's due many thousands of pounds in compensation; that ought to take the edge off his attitude.' Again he glanced out of the window. 'I was going to suggest a walk after dinner; the hotel brochure has a few local walks. But this weather . . .'

'I think you're right.' Louise D'Acre smiled and placed her hand on his. 'I think I'd appreciate an early night.'